Grayville's Story

Grayville's Story

Ron Austin

edited by
Linda Swope Austin

iUniverse LLC
Bloomington

GRAYVILLE'S STORY

This is a work of fiction. All of the characters, names, incidents,
organizations, and dialogue in this novel are either the products
of the author's imagination or are used fictitiously.

iUniverse books may be ordered through booksellers or by contacting:

iUniverse LLC
1663 Liberty Drive
Bloomington, IN 47403
www.iuniverse.com
1-800-Authors (1-800-288-4677)

Because of the dynamic nature of the Internet, any web addresses or
links contained in this book may have changed since publication and may
no longer be valid. The views expressed in this work are solely those
of the author and do not necessarily reflect the views of the publisher,
and the publisher hereby disclaims any responsibility for them.

Any people depicted in stock imagery provided by Thinkstock are
models, and such images are being used for illustrative purposes only.
Certain stock imagery © Thinkstock.

ISBN: 978-1-4917-1247-4 (sc)
ISBN: 978-1-4917-1249-8 (hc)
ISBN: 978-1-4917-1248-1 (e)

Library of Congress Control Number: 2013919555

Printed in the United States of America.

iUniverse rev. date: 12/05/2013

Preface:

In 1996 my daughter, Karen, lost ninety-two percent of her vision following surgery. To ease the pressure on my family, each evening I would share humor and high-interest stories at our dinner table. Grayville's Story grew out of this practice.

We made many trips from our home in Fayetteville, Arkansas, to the UAMS Jones Eye Institute in Little Rock, with hopes of restoring her vision. Her appointments were long, and I had hours in the waiting room. During her first appointment, I decided to write to entertain my family. I found a Primary tablet in my van and started. I wasn't trying to be a professional writer. That evening, I read to my family all I had written. When I stopped, they wanted the rest of the story. Their genuine interest told me I had to keep going. My chapter-by-chapter efforts became serial entertainment. They were enthused each time I read a chapter or revision.

After a few weeks, I began to write more seriously. I realized that a book might be attainable. My daughter was an English teacher. She began reading my work, but she died in 2000 before she could edit it. Time stresses from health issues and relocation kept the book at low priority. I wanted to self-publish; off and on for eleven years, I sought an affordable publisher. I was pleased to be readily accepted by IUniverse. I praise God for leading me to their website.

Acknowledgments:

My daughter, Karen, was my soul mate. She served as a sounding board for this book. *Shrink-wrapped Porta-Potties* was one of her contributions. She deserves the title, Contributing Author, for her attentiveness, expertise, and willingness.

I owe the most to Linda—my wife of almost 50 years—and Chip, our electrical-engineer son. This book sat unedited for years. When at last we tried to access the digital copy for editing, we realized it was missing from our computer. I had a paper copy of an old revision. [Four revisions after that were lost.] Linda offered to re-key each page into the computer. Chip figured out how to scan the copy into a Word file in editable form. For more than six months, Linda grabbed bits of time between responsibilities to edit Grayville's Story. I am creative, but without her skills this book would not have been completed.

Chapter 1

The call came at a bad time. The school secretary burst into the faculty meeting and headed straight for Karla. Karla winced, and red washed over her face and neck.

The secretary whispered to her, "You have an emergency call in the office." Karla hurried out.

But the message was overheard. The meeting became a furtive gossip game. Karla was not only a teacher on staff; she was the wife of Dean Story, president of the bank. In Grayville, as in many small towns, *anybody's* business was *everybody's* business—only more so when Dean was involved.

Apprehension pounded in her chest. She picked up the receiver. "This is Karla Story." She was shaking involuntarily and braced against her fear that this time Dean was dead.

"Mrs. Story, I'm an attorney here in Macon, Missouri Your husband is in jail."

Dean was in Little Rock on business. Karla had made his reservations at the Capitol Hotel herself. "What? That can't be. Are you sure?"

"Oh, I'm sure. That's precisely why I'm calling."

Karla knew it was Dean when she heard him muttering in the background, "I just lost control. I didn't mean to hurt her." He was being interrogated, and the man on the phone knew why.

"What happened?"

"He was operating a boat on Long Branch Lake. He ran under a private dock, and a young woman with him was severely injured. From what I hear on the local news, she was airlifted out but died en route to the hospital. Dean has been charged with negligent homicide, operating a boat under the influence of alcohol, and resisting arrest."

Her mind was reeling with questions for Dean. "What do you need me to do?"

He had done his homework. As if reading a grocery list, he said, "Go home and pack. I'll have a car there for you in forty-five minutes. The driver will take you to Fayetteville to catch American Eagle Flight 654 from Dallas. You will change planes in Columbia—Scheduled Air Taxi Flight 283. That will get you to Kirksville about three-fifteen this afternoon. I will meet you; I'm wearing a solid green shirt. We'll drive to Macon and see Dean just before visiting hours are over at five o'clock. You don't need to stop for money; just get your things. Everything is paid for. And, Dean is fine."

Karla hadn't asked about Dean. She had been down this road before. She was agonizing. "What next? Will this ever stop?" She loved Dean and was thankful he was still alive. At that moment she also wanted to wring his neck. She stepped back into the meeting room, fighting to keep her face from tattling. She felt all eyes turn as she motioned for the principal to join her in the hallway. In hushed tones, she told him about the accident and her need to leave campus. In moments she was on her way.

The attorney was right. She had only minutes with Dean. He seemed relieved she had come. She tried to be supportive. Deep within, she was weary. She was angry. She was glad when the jailor came to escort her away.

The attorney had waited. He took her to a nearby Olive Garden, where they discussed Dean's situation. Karla choked down half the lasagna she ordered. The attorney had a rental car delivered to the restaurant for her. He directed her to the motel a few blocks away where he had paid a reservation for her. He promised to do what he could for Dean.

She slept fitfully and woke much too early.

Dean had said, "Thanks for making reservations for me. One of these days, Karla, I need to take you to the Capitol Hotel for dinner. Their steaks are superb, and you know I know what I'm saying. But I'd like you to experience the service—waiters in tuxes, Karla. You deserve that. But until then, I'll be there next week enjoying it for you."

She couldn't get his deception off her mind. "How could he joke about the Capitol Hotel when he was planning to rendezvous with another woman? If he loves me, why would he do this? He's dodged the truth before, but I've never caught him in an out-and-out lie. Is this a game changer?"

She lingered in the shower, hoping the warm spray would wash away her stress. She dressed and headed for coffee in the breakfast area. She stayed for yogurt and granola then refilled her cup, grabbed a sweet roll, and went back to her room. She turned on the television and flipped channels while finishing breakfast, but she had no interest in anything that was on. Several hours stood between her and one-thirty when she could see Dean. She pulled out her diary and reached for a pen.

"August 16, 1994. Macon, Missouri. Dean is in jail again—a boating accident. He was drunk as usual.

Negligent homicide. The woman was just twenty-two.
What's he going to say this time? How can I believe him?
School starts soon. I hate losing this prep time. I'll have
to double up if Dean and I go to Washington D.C. next
weekend. Will he be out in time? Do I even want to go
now? I'm glad God is in charge."

The book was large for a diary, difficult to store
but easy to write in and read from. Karla thumbed back
through her entries. She stopped to read her comments
about Dean's trip to Alaska with his dad; she wished she
had asked more about that trip. Other entries caught
her attention. She smiled at what she had written about
Dean *hogging* catfish.

"*The water was so murky Dean couldn't even see his
hand when he reached into the hollow log. The catfish
could have been a snake! Only a daredevil has such
nerve. That fish was almost as big as a sow. There are
enough fillets to feed the booster club.*"

Reminiscing kept her occupied and settled her
nerves. Time passed quickly, and soon she was on her way
to see Dean.

Cooling your heels in a regional jail is no picnic; Dean
didn't sleep well. Late in the morning, the loudmouth in an
adjacent cell was released; and he finally relaxed into a
deep sleep. His lunch tray came, but he didn't budge. As
Karla arrived, he mumbled, "Get the 'copter. I'm ready to
leave now. The list is complete . . . ."

She couldn't make sense of his words. "Dean, what
are you talking about?"

Sleepy-eyed, he looked up. She seemed puzzled.
"What did I say, Babe?"

"I don't know, Dean. You were talking in your sleep."

"So tell me what you heard."

"*I couldn't understand you.*" She wished she had. Maybe he had said something she could use to piece things together. She loved Dean; but she had *big* questions. "Why did you come all the way up here to party? You could have done that in Little Rock for half the expense. Where were you and the girl staying? How long had you been there?" She couldn't make herself ask, "Did you have sex with her?" Tears slowly welled in her eyes and began to overflow.

Dean had answers. "I was staying at the Clarion Inn. I met her at the marina, and we went boating for a while. That's all, so quit worrying. Let's talk about this when I'm out of here."

She was jealous. And he hadn't answered all her questions. He pulled her close. She felt distant. He held her a long time, gently caressing the tension in her back. They talked until their time was up. She still wasn't at ease, but she left in a better frame of mind. As she passed from the cell block, the prison guard told Dean that his father had called. He was at the airport waiting for a taxi and would be there soon to pay his bail. She was thankful her father-in-law was still alive to help. She was glad he had come.

Dean had been adopted at the age of ten months into the home of James Dean Story. As President of First Bank of Grayville, James Dean had influence. He was well-heeled, some would say; but he didn't look it. Everyone he dealt with in the county seat respected him, except the few who had incurred his wrath. He never hesitated to use a heavy hand if Dean was vulnerable—just as executives at the Fort Smith paper had learned.

His influence with prosecutors was cash. He had money. His father had money. His grandfather made the money. And, to protect Dean, he spent money. The locals said it was old money, untouchable, accessible only by James Dean.

Dean greeted his dad with a bear hug. "Dad, I'm so glad to see you. Thank you for coming." He held him close longer than usual. He had been thinking of the many times his father had been there for him. And his concern was always Dean's welfare, not what was spent.

"Son, how are you? I see bruises. I can't believe you're not hurt worse."

"I'm fine, Dad. I'm fine. I sure appreciate you bringing the money. This place is wearing on me. I feel whipped."

The jailor was waiting. Dean put his arm around his dad's shoulder. "Let's get out of here. We can go over to Karla's room, pick her up, and head on back tonight if you like. I know you hate to run out of town on short notice and leave Mom alone."

"She's okay, Dean. Her quilting group meets tonight. But I'm tired. I'd like to get home."

Flights weren't available; home had to wait until after breakfast the next day. James Dean rose early and called his wife just after seven o'clock. She had already eaten and was finishing the newspaper. She was quick to give him the latest. "A reporter wrote a long article about Dean. She did him up well. Actually it says here she's doing a series of three articles about him. I'm so proud. The writer is Kerri Watson. Do you know her?"

James Dean stiffened. "I haven't met her. But I know her husband, Carl Lee Watson, the sports reporter. I see him at Razorback games all the time. Lay that article out for me. I want to see it."

Chapter 2

Tiny Grayville, Arkansas, nestles in the valley along
Gray River between three mountains: Panther Mountain,
Gray's Mountain, and Goat Point Mountain. Locals say
Gravel, like long-time Fayetteville residents referring
to their town as *Fedvul*. Such a nondescript location
normally would not warrant outside attention. However,
an overriding element in the history of Dean Story was
involvement of the news media.

After Dean emerged as a local leader, he made
front-page news almost every week in the *Gray Springs
County Ledger*, the hometown newspaper. He made
State news two or three times a year in the *Arkansas
Democrat/Gazette*. Usually, the articles featured his
involvement in philanthropy and public service. Not as
often, but regularly, Dean's name was linked to casualties.
Despite the media bird-dogging his role in these
tragedies, mystery prevailed. Grayville locals told one
version, the media another. Only those assigned to the
Bridge knew the truth.

Dean's lifestyle—in and out of the shadows—might
have stayed under the radar except for the wiles of an
energetic young reporter named Kerri Watson. Kerri
and her husband, Carl Lee, were both reporters for the
Arkansas Democrat-Gazette. They met during the press
war of the late 1980's and the early 1990's, won by the
Arkansas Democrat. Kerri had worked for the *Arkansas
Gazette*. Carl Lee was a sportswriter for the *Arkansas
Democrat*. Their mutual interests fueled a whirlwind
courtship, and they married six months later.

When Kerri came on staff with the *Democrat*, the
news editor had given her a unique assignment. "Get out
there and see what's happening. Dig back a few months.

Read every newspaper you can get your hands on. Search the major news outlets, and watch news on television. Spend two weeks with your ears and eyes open. Don't write articles, just consume and process information, keeping notes on whatever catches your attention. Then come see me."

Kerri put her heart into her work. She pored over newspapers. She tuned into every news channel and radio station. The days ticked away. Her long hours emptied a bottle of artificial tears. Finally, she was ready to see the editor.

His deep bellowing bass voice beckoned. "Good morning, Kerri. Come in and have a seat."

"Good morning, sir." She perched daintily on a massive armchair. "You told me to report after two weeks. Here I am; and I have lots of notes."

The editor responded to her energy. He seemed already glad she had come aboard. "I hope you enjoyed your research. Now, I want you to go to the conference room down the hall. Organize what you've gleaned from your media immersion. Form ideas about news interests you would like to pursue. I will join you in an hour."

In the conference room, she set to work, flipping pages on her yellow pad as she went. She had a master's degree in journalism. She had been thorough. Three main categories emerged: accidental deaths, politics, and lawsuits/legal matters. She breathed silently to the empty room, "This can't be true." A man named Dean Story was common to all three. He was tied to accidental deaths in articles in the *Arkansas Democrat/Gazette*, the Russellville *Courier*, the *Gray Springs County Ledger*, and the Memphis *Commercial Appeal.* He was named multiple times in reports on legal issues and politics.

She was ready when the editor joined her. She told him of her discovery. "This guy stokes my curiosity. Is he reckless or just accident prone? How does he always land on his feet? Does he know every lawmaker in the nation? I don't know if I've hit on a story or not, but he has my attention."

Her enthusiasm drew him in. "I like your ideas, Kerri. In fact, I've locked in on Dean Story myself. I have a sizable file on him. You can start there. Here's a key to my cabinet. It's not Mullins at the U of A, but everything is alphabetical and cross-indexed. You shouldn't have trouble pulling what you need."

The editor was a walking encyclopedia. He was a great writer, conservative and somewhat idiosyncratic in his discussion of politics. She had idolized his style long before the *Gazette* was gobbled up by the *Democrat.* She was eager to see his records. "Great. I'm ready, sir."

That evening, she told her husband about the editor's approach and how she found a topic. He thought, "That's my Kerri, the master sleuth, always aligning facts to get the truth. Like a hound sniffing out bones, she's all over any issue she tackles. She should have been a trial lawyer." He was impressed with the editor's initiation process.

"So, what did you decide?"

"I chose a guy named Dean Story from Grayville in northwest Arkansas.

"Hey, I've met that guy. He's at all the Razorback games. He's one heck-of-a-fan! You ought to see him in action. He enters Walton Arena like a dignitary—pumping hands, back-slapping the guys, and hugging the girls. When the band strikes up, he's out of his seat yelling, *Woo Pig Sooie! Razorbacks!*"

"Are you sure that's the same person?"

"Karla, I'm absolutely sure. You just haven't seen him in action. One night when the Razorback mascot came repelling down from the upper decks to the court, Dean ran down the aisle, across the south end of the court, and was halfway up the rope before two honcho security officials grabbed the rope and coaxed him back down. He was already a stand-out in his red hat, shirt, and boots—looking good with white jeans. When his feet hit the floor, he did a quick pirouette; and his hat was off to the rousing ovation of the crowd. He two-stepped a cheerleader to the media table and shook hands with the folks there on his way back to his seat—smack dab in the middle of the student section.

Dean is a composite of Hoss Cartwright the TV cowboy, and my cousin Carroll Lee Austin, the banjo-picking singer dude from Pine Bluff. He is *Mr. Excitement, Mr. Energy* like the Hog Wild Band director who moved to Louisiana Tech—the one you said crooned like Dean Martin. You couldn't pick a more interesting topic, Kerri. Go for it."

From then on, she picked up on every issue involving Dean, however trivial or personal. His father accused her of having a personal goal to discredit Dean and twice tried to have her fired. He filed suit against her, and the case was dismissed as frivolous. But James Dean was not far from the truth.

When she began the series on Dean, her first article read as if she were nominating him for an outstanding youth award. At various points she showed that he had budded early.

> Dean was at the top of the pecking order by the time he was ten years old.
>
> ....
>
> From junior high through high school, he was the *go-to-guy* in basketball, the spark that fired up the team. He always energized the crowd when he got the ball on either end; he either fouled or got fouled fifteen to twenty times a game. He led the conference in two categories: fouls and free-throws attempted. He was a natural wit. He joked around during practices and games; but his team won—thirty-two and one his senior year.
>
> ....
>
> After high school, he worked two years for a senator in Washington, D.C.

The only hint of negative was her report about a couple incidents in Dean's college years. But her real intention for the series was revealed after the article was printed.

The editor had called her to his office. He was beaming. "Fine article, Kerri! What are you planning for Part Two?"

"I'm analyzing the background of those whose deaths involved Dean. I want to know if there is a connection. And I'm checking on the significance of the rescue helicopter that's always involved."

"Do you have photos?"

"I have sent the Associated Press more than thirty requests for photo enlargements with computer enhancement, so I can make out the details. I'd like to see who else may be in the pictures and fix the exact location of as many shots as possible."

He smiled broadly. "Kerri, you are doing a fine job. Stay on the trail; you might have the story of the year. Just keep the facts straight."

Chapter 3

As a little girl, Kerri was sure her mother had eyes in back of her head. She seemed to always know what Kerri was doing. When questioned about her omniscience, she would tease, "A little bird told me." Such a bird would have served Kerri well the day Karla learned about Dean's mess up in Macon.

After the principal told his faculty why Karla was leaving, the room grew quiet—unnaturally quiet. Many of the teachers were thinking, "This guy is new. He doesn't realize this isn't Dean's first crisis." When he couldn't move past this disconnect, he postponed the meeting until the next day. He gave them the remaining hours to work in their rooms.

For two who were Karla's friends, work would wait. "Can you believe Dean's messed up again?"

"No. I feel sorry for Karla! Our new principal knows nothing about Dean and how she has been impacted. Don't you think we should tell him at least enough to understand her situation?"

"I sure do." They headed down the hall.

The principal was at his desk reworking the agenda. He invited them in. "Have a seat. How may I help you ladies?"

"We would like to share some of Grayville's history with you. Considering today's disruption, we think you should know about Karla's husband."

"I would appreciate that. May I offer you a soda or some coffee?"

Drinks were arranged as the women settled into chairs near his desk. A mere twenty-five minutes after the abrupt adjournment, the teachers were into their mission, with stories flowing in rapid succession. Sometimes both talked at once. At other times, one talked a while; then the other picked up the story and went right on. As they relived events in Dean's life, they talked as if they were actually part of the action. Some stories were exaggerated to make Dean look good. Others were changed to protect him.

"Dean is really a nice guy. He has a caring attitude, and folks know they can count on him in a pinch. He will do whatever he can to help anyone. He visits the homes of bereaved families and attends funerals and weddings. He weeps unashamedly because he truly cares. He gets around town shaking hands, punching the men on the shoulder, or forearming them—as a boy might—just to let them know he is there. He always has a hug for unattached women; but he offers a mannerly tip of the hat, nod, or handshake when he meets a married lady. He is liked by everyone in town."

The office doors were closed. Piped-in music muffled sound. Their conversation could not be heard outside—except for an occasional laugh, or a loud "He did what?" Their coffee cups would be refilled twice as the history rambled from one teacher to the other.

Working in the Capitol matured Dean. The teenager returned home a man. The postmaster was vocal with his assessment. "His eyes are focused when he listens to you, and his posture is so neutralizing."

To prepare Dean to follow him as head of Grayville's bank, his father sent him to college. Arkansas Tech in Russellville became his new place of residence. That's where he met Karla. They dated frequently early on, but their relationship progressed slowly.

Karla was preoccupied. Her mother died during her freshman year, and she frequently traveled home to help with her younger siblings. Her brother was in his senior year of high school; her sister was a ninth-grader. Being needed helped her grief. Her sophomore year was better until her father grew ill and died within three months. She told Dean, "He had lung cancer. He went so quickly once it was found. I could tell he suffered, but he didn't complain. Missing Mom was all he talked about. He was so lonely after she died."

Karla was a slight young woman but mature for her age. What she lacked in size, she made up for with fixed resolve. She never flinched at taking responsibility for her brother and sister. They had always been close, and the loss of their parents deepened this bond. Limited finances required the sale of their family home. Karla rented an apartment for them near campus. Her brother had already committed to the ROTC program at Tech. Her sister transferred to Russellville High School.

Karla continued to see Dean, eventually giving him exclusive rights to her date time. But she struggled with her growing affection for him. His lifestyle of adventure made her uneasy. "Dean would have to settle down to marry me. I couldn't handle him always taking risks."

In his sophomore year, Dean moved into an apartment with friends—Jake Tullis from Dallas and twins from Fort Smith. Dean had tagged them Bubba and Dubba Bubba at first sight.

Jake was enrolled in Tech's pre-med program. He qualified to pay his tuition with the G.I. Bill by serving five years in the U.S. Marine Corps. His last two years in the military were spent on special assignment at the Earle Cabell Federal Building in Dallas. There he happened onto paperwork regarding salvaged aircraft parts sold to the military as rebuilt parts. At the time, he assumed the issue was under investigation and didn't give his discovery further thought.

However, the officials he thought were handling the situation were actually involved in the scam. When they were charged with fraud, he realized the significance of his discovery. He had accessed evidence. Though he knew nothing beyond what was already public, he was on the radar of their cohorts. To dodge them and their pressure, he decided against reenlistment and enrolled at Tech.

The case came to court, and on a Wednesday the jury reached their verdict: Guilty! Jake learned about the outcome that Thursday when he stopped by his home after a track meet. His father told him, "Pressure will be a hundred-fold now. Keep cool. I will arrange to get you out of town to isolate you from those guys. I'll call you Saturday."

But back at campus, Jake began to drink on Friday— and heavily. He and his friends were into their usual betting on sporting events. The wagers were always small and mostly for entertainment. They were good at ragging the losers. Wins had always been hit and miss, so all of them were surprised when Jake hit a winning streak on pro basketball.

Saturday arrived, but daylight was hours away. Outside Dean's apartment, the policeman ordered, "You'll have to wait outside the crime-scene banner, sir." The reporter stressed, "Captain, I'm with the *Courier*. I was sent to cover the shooting incident, and I need to get in to do my job."

The policeman didn't budge. He was following protocol. The campus was not subject to freedom of information laws. The student apartments were off campus, but Security from Arkansas Tech had jurisdiction according to a reciprocal agreement with local law enforcement officials. The policeman interpreted that to mean reporters were not allowed at the site without a release by the school.

The reporter didn't give up. He was just starting out, and he doubled in route delivery. He knew the address. The guys involved in the incident were his customers. He walked back to his truck and pilfered through his glove compartment. He came up with his record book and their names. He headed across I-40. Many students had stayed on campus for the weekend because of the track meet. The Waffle House was one of the few twenty-four hour hangouts. Students were there after midnight.

Luck was with him. He spotted the twins who roomed with Dean and Jake at a table alone. They looked like they had been traumatized. Their eyes were red and puffy. He asked if he could join them. They simply nodded and pointed to an empty chair. As he sat down he asked, "What happened? No one from the paper is allowed to get in, and we have no story. Could you give me some information?" They needed to unload. The reporter was someone to talk to; they agreed. They choked up occasionally as they alternated giving him details.

"We make a game of betting on weekends—just small change. Jake Tullis hit every bet Friday in addition to some dollar bets on the track meet the day before. He told us he felt invulnerable. Each time he learned about another win, he asked one of us to add a bullet to the cylinder of his old family Colt 45 heirloom and spin it. And each time he feinted pulling the trigger saying, 'Bam!' and boasting, 'I'm still here.'

When he had hit seven in a row, he exclaimed, 'Wow! I'm gonna pull the trigger on this one. I can't be beat.' He asked us to remove all but one bullet from the cylinder. He shoved his Arkansas Tech Wonder Boys cap toward us and said, 'Drop the extras in here, and then spin it. I'll show you just how lucky I am.'

We heard what Jake asked us to do. We had been drinking too, but we made sure *all* the bullets went into the cap. He counted them and yelled, 'I said, all but one!' Then he hollered, 'Hey, go get our cooler. We need something to drink. I think we done run through yours.' There were two cases of beer iced down in Dean's vehicle. We're neither one super strong, and we knew both of us would be needed to carry it up the stairs. We headed out to the parking lot. It was about six-thirty.

Dean had been dealing with a hangover all day. He drank a six-pack between four and five o'clock and fell asleep soon after. Jake's yelling aroused him from his stupor. He told us that he awoke hearing him shout, 'All but one!' After we left he asked what he meant. Jake said, 'Bullets, Dean—bullets.' So he grabbed the gun and filled all cylinders but one.

A foggy mental state will dumb you down. Most everyone knows the traditional Russian roulette game— put one bullet in the cylinder, spin, and fire. Dean was really soused, or he would have realized what Jake meant. He told us afterward, 'I felt as if I was in slow motion when he grabbed the gun, held it to his head, and fired.'

Wailing sirens awakened Karla. The sound was too fresh a memory. A tear rolled down her cheek. She glanced at her clock—two-fifteen in the morning. "Lord, please be with whoever needs that ambulance. And I need your comfort. I am so dependent on you. Please bless my family. Dean needs your hand on him, too. Amen." She relaxed into her pillow. Before she could drift off, the phone rang. She was startled. "Who could be calling in the middle of the night?" Hesitantly, she lifted the receiver and quietly said, "Hello."

On the other end, a man introduced himself as an attorney. "Miss Barnes, Dean Story asked me to call you. He's in Polk County Regional Jail."

She was instantly more alert. She sat up on the side of her bed. "You have to be joking. Dean said he was going home after the track meet."

"This is no joke, Miss Barnes. He is charged with negligence in the shooting of Jake Tullis late yesterday. The policeman said something about Dean tampering with a gun."

She suddenly felt chilled and pulled the bed covers back over her legs. "Why did you call me? What can I do?"

"Dean has had a rough night. He's pretty shook up. He insisted I ask you to come. Do you know how to get here?"

"Yes." She thought quickly about obligations for the day ahead. "I'll be there in less than an hour." She showered quickly. The moisture drew her ash brown hair into frizzy curls. She preferred it straight, but she didn't have time to fuss with it. She slipped on jeans and a T-shirt and threw make-up into her large leather bag with the thirty-inch shoulder strap. Leaving a note for her sister, she dashed out to her car and drove across town. At red lights she worked through her make-up routine, which she kept simple for a natural look.

When she reached Dean, he was trembling. He whimpered, "I didn't mean to kill him. I thought he told me to put bullets in all but one cylinder, so that's what I did. I was half asleep and half drunk. I didn't know he was planning to pull the trigger." He cried; he had broken down several times. He clung to Karla. He promised he would never drink, gamble, *cuss*, or play with guns ever again. He just wanted to get out and go home. And she believed him.

James Dean's sleep was disrupted by a phone call. He knew what to do. A transaction of this sort had to be done quickly, quietly, smoothly, and in cash. He opened his safe.

He had a long-standing practice of stashing away money. This began in 1949, with about twenty dollars a month. As he managed his cows better, they were more productive; and he pocketed increasing amounts. For two years he had been setting back almost five grand a month. He did not tithe this money. He figured it would be tithed at his death, if there was any left after he raised Dean. He knew his son.

As he listened in the dark, there was a quiet tap at his back door. He handed Dean's attorney a sack with thirty thousand dollars in hundreds and twenties, unmarked and nearly uncirculated.

Bail was set at two hundred thousand dollars. The prosecutor didn't want Dean to get out. The word would get around campus. He held a hard line on reckless behavior—no copycat crime on his watch.

But he mellowed. The next day, Dean's attorney slipped him a used bulky brown envelope. The prosecutor put the crumpled parcel inside a "Wally World" plastic bag from a morning purchase. He casually laid the bag on his credenza to count later—fifteen thousand in twenty dollar bills, unmarked and nontaxable. Not even his wife would know about this. He told himself it was only right to drop the charges. Who could deny the convincing testimony of those twins?

Chapter 4

The following summer passed quickly. Dean spent five weekends in Dallas with the Tullis family, attending church and dining out afterward. Jake had been his close friend. The family's grief was heavy on him. They had forgiven him—immediately after the funeral. Their healing was slow, but he could tell they were coming along.

The last Sunday Dean was with them in church, several people came forward in response to the sermon. The pastor introduced them and told the congregation about their decisions. A young couple had become debt free and wanted to thank God publicly. Three others came to profess faith in Jesus Christ as Savior. One of those renounced his habits of gambling and drinking. Still others came for church membership or baptism.

The audience applauded, and then the pastor asked everyone to be seated. Instead of giving the closing prayer as usual he said, "Someone has asked permission to address a family in our church with you as witnesses. This is not customary, but I think the Lord would be pleased. Dean Story, come up here and stand by me brother."

Dean walked from the front pew and threw his big arms around the pastor. He said, "I love you. Your patient counseling and prayer support have given me courage to do what I have to do today. Thank you." He squared his shoulders, stood straight up with his hands to his side, and looked out over the more than two thousand gathered that day—members, guests and visitors.

"On the evening of May 20, I was sleeping off a hangover. I halfway awoke, still mostly drunk, and put seven bullets in a Colt 45. I gave the cylinder a spin, pulled back the hammer, and gave the gun to Jake Tullis, my roommate. He used that gun to shoot himself. My stupidity and carelessness permanently changed this family.

The past four months have been the longest and hardest I have lived. I know God was not pleased with me. I have repented and asked for forgiveness. Not only did God forgive me; so did the Tullis family. They are here today, and I would like them to join me down front for a moment."

Silence draped the room. Tears flowed as Jake's family made their way to the front. Dean's humility and the family's forgiveness impacted those present. One teen whispered to her father, "I love you, Daddy. Please forgive me for the way I've been acting." There were hugs between parents, parents and children, friends, and strangers. People reached out to touch neighbors down the pews. Many held hands with those sitting beside them.

From somewhere in back rose a pure first tenor voice. "When peace, like a river attendeth my way, when sorrows like sea billows roll . . . ." As the melody continued, all over the church one by one people rose and crossed the aisles in an almost continuous chain of hands. The tenor voice was everywhere now. Who and where the singer was didn't seem to matter. No one spent time searching. Those who knew the words joined him. An old black grandma shouted at the top of her lungs, "It is well here today. Praise the Lord!" Her husband said, "Uh huh, I know that's right."

It was well with Dean, and it was well with Jake's family. They had forgiven him. He spoke with each one. He embraced them all, weeping. Afterward, they all turned toward the congregation arm in arm. The light revealed tears, but peace radiated from each face. A second verse began. This time nearly two thousand voices ended the chorus with a resounding, "It is well. It is well with my soul."

Karla's former roommate at Tech was from Grayville, and that summer Karla frequented her home on weekends— mostly when Dean would be home. When the weather was nice, the girls would ride four-wheelers to the river behind her folks' small barn. The river, which snaked along their property line, provided recreation for swimmers, boaters, picnicking families, and boys fishing from the bank. Karla and her friend would meander along the bank, relishing the fresh air and their time together. More often than not, they encountered Dean.

Karla was in town the weekend of the Boy Scout fund-raising event. Dean was all over the place: cheering on sack-racers, pulling for his toad-frog to leap to victory out of the circle in the dirt, and singing enthusiastically off-key for children clustered around him. He bellowed, "I'm bringing home a baby bumblebee. Won't my mommy be so proud of me . . . ." and the kids joined in.

Late morning, just before hotdogs were served, Dean rode sitting backward on a mule all the way to the river and back. The crowd cheered as he careened haphazardly along the rocky trail without tumbling off. Then the macho man unashamedly bowed before his admirers, doffing his football helmet adorned with a bicycle mirror.

In the shade nearby, two sixty-something matrons in retro aluminum folding chairs had been having a high time watching him. When they could stop laughing, one said, "Dean will do anything to raise money. You'd never catch me trying that. Three and a half miles on a mule is enough to wear out the sitting place on even a fat man! His rear is bigger than any woman's on the square. He's got to be at least a size extra, extra large. He definitely fills his jeans."

"Yeah, he does; but he's solid. There's not much fat there. He works out all the time." Glancing sideways, she cautioned, "We better hush up. Here comes his dad. He wouldn't like us talking about Dean that-a-way." They smiled and greeted James Dean, then scurried away for a hot dog and pop.

Dean and Karla became an item that summer. Grayville residents got to know her and began to discuss Dean's obvious infatuation. One inquired, "How long's she been comin' around?" Another who kept up with such things noted, "Seems to me Dean is falling for her." Talk about Dean occasionally included the gun incident with Jake Tullis, but never in the presence of the new couple.

Fall came, and football season began. Dean and Karla had fun on road trips to follow the Wonder Boys to UCA in Conway, Henderson at Arkadelphia, and UAPB in Pine Bluff. Tech won often, and that meant parties. Dean began to drink again, even with Karla present. He *cussed* and swore at the officials and bet on a few professional sporting events. Otherwise, he stayed out of trouble.

That November, Daniel Penzo hosted Dean on his first duck hunt: five days at Fish-Lake Slough, just off I-40 near Brinkley, deep in the wild wetlands of a Cache River backwater holding area and flood waters of the White River. Ducks, lots of ducks, landed there first, due to the permanent water habitat.

Dean met Dan at Boys' State the summer after their junior year in high school. That led to Dan spending two weekends with Dean in Grayville. Early in the fall of their senior year, they went together to Washington, D.C., for a three-day seminar. Their friendship was unique because basically they were opposites. Science, computers, and photography were interests of Dan. Dean was a sportsman risk-taking cowboy populist "wanna-be" political king-maker. But Dan knew duck hunting.

In rural eastern Arkansas, duck hunting is a traditional winter pastime. Large-acre farms, stilled by cold weather, wait for spring and new crop loans. After equipment maintenance is done, farmers take to their fields for recreation. Each duck season, locals are joined by more than six thousand hunters from outside the county—in Dean's heyday, a million dollar annual boost to the economy.

Motels were always full, and there were numerous duck clubs. Large clubs could accommodate more than two hundred hunters per week, averaging two days of hunting per man. Hunting attire ranged from simple, low-cost wear of the working class and students to matching, stylish, expensive outfits of wealthy planters, ginners, businessmen, professional sportsmen, elected officials, and other dignitaries. Video cameras brought along also reflected the affluence, or lack thereof, of the photographers wielding them.

The morning of a hunt, clubs were a beehive of activity: checking equipment, loading shell vests and cases, filling thermoses with coffee, and pulling on camouflage suits. The ritual included an early feast of biscuits, gravy, bacon or sausage, fried eggs, grits, and coffee—topped off with a huge home-made cinnamon roll.

Then four-wheel-drive vehicles would silently parade past frozen fields to the duck blinds.

The two friends unloaded their gear in a *not so choice* motel—thirty-six rooms and a covert gambling hall that in five minutes, on cue, could transform into a *mom and pop* cafe complete with tables of half-eaten food. Hard mattresses made for good sleeping—for the lucky who could tune out an occasional idling FBL or International Haulers transport truck.

The parking lot hosted trucking names not often seen on Arkansas highways. Dean couldn't figure why a trucker with a top-of-the-line sleeper in his rig would check in at the motel. He didn't know about the Memphis girls who held three suites down on the far wing. With their base C.B. radio, they connected with *dates.* Truckers awaiting trip orders would detour for a lay-over. Their employers paid the expenses, so they kept good company.

Dean and Dan awoke at five each morning, were dressed and in the blinds by six-thirty, and shot their limit each day. Rigorous outings and Dean's appetite led to hearty meals at the Mallard Club Restaurant, Field's Diner, and the truck stop at Brinkley. Dean was an instant fan of the sport and the cuisine. He was so fired up afterward that he got Dan to commit to take him again. But Dean headed for D.C. after high school, and their plan was set aside.

Chapter 5

Dean and Dan stayed in touch. Dean's senior year at Tech, he invited Dan to Homecoming. Karla lined up a date for him, and they all had a great weekend together. While reliving their duck hunt for the girls—who weren't especially impressed, they decided to take their plans off hold and hit the duck waters again. Dean suggested that the twins from Fort Smith join them for a foursome. Dan agreed, saying the extra weight in the boat would help if they encountered ice. Dean set the outing for Dead Day—a day of no classes set aside to study for final tests.

To be free on Dead Day cost them three days of cramming for finals beforehand, with barely five hours sleep a night. On their first night away from campus, all sacked out by nine o'clock. The next morning Dean shouted, "Wake up, dudes!" as he left the bathroom; the twins groaned in unison. After a few minutes he headed downstairs to warm up the Jeep, shouting over his shoulder, "Let's get it on. The ducks are out there eating those beans, just waiting for us." Bubba and Dubba Bubba jumped out of bed, hit the shower, dressed, and met Dean at his Cherokee. They picked up boats at Lake Conway, stopped at Anderson's Grill in Beebe for breakfast, and reached the flooded bean fields before shooting hours.

Dan rose earlier than his friends. He had packed the night before: flashlight, warm clothes, food, pop, plastic ware, cups, shells, gun, knife, first-aid kit, waders, pillow, and allergy pills. Without consulting Dean, he had picked up a case of *Bud* on his way home from Pine Bluff.

He faced a two-hour drive from his home in Fordyce. His headlights traced two-lane roads to Hazen, past Des Arc to County Road 323, then right on 36, ten miles southeast of West Point, almost to Georgetown. His father had been raised due east of there in White County in the productive fields along the White River. In the fifties and sixties, the area's patchwork of two-thousand-acre family farms was bought up by farm management companies which transformed them into corporate farms ten townships in size. To the northeast, the natural habitat was maximized into the Hurricane Lake Wildlife Management Area.

When he arrived, the others were already at water's edge—the boats launched and gear loaded. He caught the aroma of coffee before he could recognize their faces in the dark. Hoisting a thermos, Dean shouted, "How 'bout a cup, little guy?" A cold front had passed through during the night. Ice was already forming around bean tops sticking through the water. A harsh wind blew across the open fields. Dan downed a whole cup of warmth without his usual cream and sugar.

Tanked up with caffeine, they launched onto an area of flooded beans more than three-and-a-half miles wide and seven miles long. In a place or two, land poked through the water like islands. The service road and river were on the north and east, high ground on the south and west. Ice cracked, sounding like distant cloud-to-cloud lightning, distinct and eerie, as the four ran their twelve-foot boat up on the ice to break it. This made a path for the larger sixteen-foot river boat, loaded with gear and three hunters—the twins and Dan. They were on their way; Dean was in the smaller boat, leading as usual. Slow-going through the thin ice ate up forty-five minutes before they reached a point out far enough to set up a decent floating blind.

Frozen into place, like objects painted on a canvas, the two boats lay quiet as ducks grew closer and closer. Dean stood up, poking his gun through the slits in the boat cover. Dan said, "Sit down, man, you're gonna run the ducks out of the county." Dean promptly sat down; Dan had cautioned them once before.

Shooting at a mallard, hitting a wood duck, shooting at another mallard, looking for signs of a hit, and the morning's hunt was on. Soon all of them were into the fun. Dean joked, "Flood it and they will come." He was right. They all laughed.

Time passed quickly. The sun, still hiding behind thickening clouds, was barely evident almost overhead. Dan counted their haul, "Four mallards, two wood ducks, and a pintail. I would say that's pretty good hunting for beginners."

Bubba responded, "Hey, look at the time. It's twelve-twenty. I'm hungry as a bear. Let's go eat." He pulled out the ax to cut ice that had refrozen about a quarter inch thick around the boats. He shivered. A little further out, ice had thickened to about half an inch. The temperature had dropped, and the lull in activity was emphasizing the cold.

Dubba Bubba, in front, slowly turned the big boat around with the small paddle, trolling like a fisherman. He was so smooth and careful that the others hardly sensed the motion. Dean grabbed the rope tied to the small boat, gave it a big tug, and spun it around in one quick motion to follow the big boat out. But leaving the water was not that easy. They reached dry ground just before one-thirty, pulled the boats out, and headed for warmth and nourishment in the Cherokee. Their ducks were almost frozen; there would be no field-dressing. Dan said, "Throw 'em in the cooler and let's eat."

Country/western music played quietly over the background hum of the Jeep's engine. Four big appetites ravaged through bags of food. After lunch, leftovers were tossed in the back with other supplies. Full stomachs took over. Three of the hunters were soon snoozing in their captain's chairs.

But Dean spotted the Bud while rummaging for chips and drank *a few* as he would later confess. Meanwhile, temperature and wind factor combined to thicken the ice to nearly three-quarters of an inch. The ducks were also thicker and more desperate for food. As the hunters roused, droves of ducks honed in on bean-laden stalks peeking through and held fast by the icecap.

Ducks, from the horizon to within a stone's throw, reinvigorated the hunters. They eagerly headed back out. Adrenaline masked the deep chill. Noise from high rpm attempts to motor the small boat onto the ice disturbed the feeding frenzy for only seconds. The ducks settled again. Downy feathers floated and flittered across the ice—moist smelly feathers sticking and freezing upright on the bean sea.

The six-section *lake* on which they floated hid the skeleton of the field below. On the north side was a road which spanned the field, beyond which lay another flooded five sections. Parallel irrigation ditches followed the road. These were intersected by south-running ditches. Across these, farmers had positioned old railroad flatcars as bridges to move equipment from side to side.

The hunters found it impossible to navigate to their original spot. Dan's Walkman was tuned to local radio station KWCK; he heard the report, *twenty-five degrees*. He cautioned, "Stick close to the edge and toward the road. That might be our best path through the ice. And be careful. We can't afford to get wet; we'd freeze in five minutes."

Dan weighed just over half what Dean weighed, and the twins each weighed only slightly more than Dan. Dean was the only one heavy enough to ride the small boat through the ice. Eventually, even he was unable to break through and move further out. He said, "I may need some help here. But first, I'm gonna try something." He stepped onto the back end cap and throttled the ten-horse motor. He yelled, "Oh! Oh! Oh! I'm going airborne."

The front of the boat stood at a forty-five degree angle, locked in place. Dean leaned slowly toward the front, and the boat settled some but remained thirty degrees out of level. Beneath the surface, it teetered on a flatcar bridge.

Chapter 6

A frantic message hit the airwaves, "Breaker, one-nine, breaker, one-nine. We have an emergency and need an ambulance immediately. Anybody out there, do you copy?"

A trucker out of Brinkley picked up the call on his CB radio. "Go ahead, Breaker. I've got you."

"We're in a Cherokee headed toward Searcy on Highway 36, about fourteen miles south."

The trucker relayed the message through a base station in McCrory to the Central Emergency Service in Searcy. They intercepted an ambulance returning from Griffithville, only a few miles away.

When the Cherokee reached the community of West Point, the ambulance was waiting at the *T* intersection of Highways 323 and 36. Emergency lights were flashing, and white-clad attendants stood ready by the rear door. But the intended patient didn't ride in the ambulance. The trucker's relay call had been overheard, and an *air ambulance* had been dispatched from Little Rock for him. The wind whipped loudly as it descended, swirling loose snow into the faces of bystanders. Green clad EMT's quickly stabilized the injured man and loaded him inside. As the helicopter lifted, the ambulance attendants were loading another hunter from the Jeep.

No one at the scene had ever witnessed a medical air evacuation. Some had never even seen an ambulance in their rural community, so the helicopter's size and color seemed insignificant. One local who watched from the

West Point Store simply noted, "It shore was a biggun, wadden it?" Somber faces nodded agreement.

The ambulance came to an abrupt stop at the hospital emergency entrance. The Jeep quickly wheeled up behind. Red lights from the ambulance flashed intermittently on the pavement. The hunters were hustled through double glass doors into bright light.

The local sheriff had been waiting at the hospital and observed their arrival. He made a notation that all the hunters were wet through and through, with frozen patches on their coats and pants. As he made other entries for his report, an attendant approached. "They're all in the ER. Two are okay; they're warming up under blankets. We're working with the big guy."

Dean was a crust of muddy ice. Bean stalk fragments and leaves were embedded in his hair and plastered in the crevices of his clothing. He shook the attendants off, refusing treatment. He seemed frantic. "Let me go. I've got to check on Dan. Somebody tell me he's okay. Don't any of you know anything? Oh, God, help him. I did my best to get him up quickly. Don't frigid temperatures sometimes help people survive?"

The sheriff opted to talk first to the twins. As he entered their room, they searched his face. Their hearts were pounding, their eyes begging for good news. Their ashen faces were streaked with tears. He introduced himself and showed them his badge. They responded with their names and told him they were suite-mates with Dean at Tech. He sat across from them. "Can you tell me what happened?"

Both started talking at once. They were hyper, intense—adrenaline rushing as it had when the accident occurred. "Everything happened so quickly. We didn't have time to think. We reacted. We were just trying to save Dan."

"Take it easy, I'm not here to accuse anybody. Help me piece this together."

"We had been on the ice hunting duck all morning. After lunch, we tried to get back out to the same spot. The ice was thicker. Dean's boat got stuck. He moved to the back and started the motor. Suddenly, the front of the boat flew up out of the water. Dean moved until he was standing on the middle seat of the boat. The front was three feet off the water; the back was rammed through the ice.

Dan eased onto the back of the boat to help Dean push through the ice. There he was, sitting on one end of that *teeter-totter* when Dean shouted, 'Geronimo!' and leaped from the middle seat. He landed one knee on the front seat and the other leg on the floor in the very front. His two-hundred sixty-two pounds slammed the front of the boat down with such thrust that Dan catapulted over his head and into the water—feet first, gun in hand, sucking air, and wheezing.

We knew Dean had drunk more than a six-pack. We hoped he would stay put. But he was in the water before either of us could react. He fought through the tangle of frozen stalks and found Dan. He pulled him up, and together we were able to flip him onto the sixteen-footer. Dean was scrambling to climb in. Thankfully—with what help he could muster—we managed to drag him aboard.

By this time, we were wet too. We remembered the trash bags brought to hold our ducks and slipped them over all our bodies; we were terrified of freezing. The coffee in our thermos wasn't scalding, so we poured it over Dan's clothing while Dean gave him mouth-to-mouth. We cut the little boat loose and started the Evinrude. I don't know how we got that boat through the ice. I guess the combined weight of us all made a difference.

We had a major struggle to get Dan from the boat into the Cherokee. Then we cranked it, turned on the heater, and drove toward the road. Dean was in the back trying to do CPR—breathe, breathe, breathe, push—again and again. We were all too cold to think, and we weren't sure of the rate or frequency required. At one point Dan's leg twitched, and we thought he was coming around. But that was his only response, though Dean gave it all he had."

The sheriff asked the twins to submit to tests for blood alcohol and drugs. They agreed without hesitation. As he finished his entries, a tech arrived from the lab. He left to take a statement from Dean.

After a short while, he returned. He stood silent a few seconds, slowly turning his head to look both boys in the eye. "I just received a radio report from the helicopter. The other hunter with you was dead before they reached the hospital. I'm sorry. You boys can leave, but your friend will have to go with me. He's been charged with negligent homicide."

Disbelief poured over them. Finally, the truth registered; and their heads dropped. Sorrow gripped them, first for Dan, then for Dean. Alcohol had pulled him under again.

Ron Austin

Karla was taking in the six o'clock news while waiting for cheese to bubble on pizza in the oven. The phone's long loud ring drowned the reporter's announcement, "Duck hunting accident claims the life of a Fordyce man this afternoon. We'll have details at ten."   She jumped up and grabbed the receiver.

"Hello."

"Is this Karla Barnes?"

"Yes."

"I'm calling you from Searcy. I'm an attorney representing Dean Story. He is in jail and asked me to contact you."

"No! *No!* He told me he was going hunting with some buddies. What happened?"

"He is charged in the death of one of them. His friend was thrown from their boat. Dean pulled him out, but hypothermia had already taken a toll."

Karla wasn't getting it. "So, why was Dean charged?"

"I really don't have time to discuss everything now. Can you come? He's not handling this well and says he needs you."

"I'll leave in fifteen minutes."

He gave her driving directions. "I will meet you at the Roadrunner. I'm driving a white Dodge Dakota 4x4 pickup. You'll see my flashers."

"I've got it. I'll be there soon." She knelt on the spot. "Oh God, my Father, I need your strength. Please give me words to comfort Dean. How many times have I called? You are always there. This time I am asking something extra for him. His Dad will bail him out, and the trouble will go away legally. I want more, something only you can give—grace, grace to ask forgiveness, to grow, and to live triumphantly in the middle of this crisis. I know Dean is wild and a risk-taker. He brings problems on himself; only you can fix that. Lord, I love Dean. Help me to understand him . . . ." She shifted from a carpet ridge that was cutting into her knee. Her prayer went on more than five minutes.

She wrapped crumpled foil around a couple pieces of pizza, stashed the rest in the fridge, grabbed a Sunkist and her jacket, and hurried to her car. She ate on the way and still made record time. In minutes she was meeting with Dean's attorney and the sheriff. She listened carefully as they talked. They mentioned Dean's blood alcohol level.

She couldn't believe what she heard. "Eighteen percent . . . ? Are you sure the test was accurate? That's a high level."

"The tests are ninety-nine and a half percent accurate; they are done in the hospital's pathology lab. Computers now do the analyses. There's no human error."

The men talked about Dean's attempt to save Dan. Karla heard *heroic, courageous,* and *brave.* They admitted he outdistanced their abilities.

"I couldn't have done what he did."

"I doubt I could have either. Someone wearing only a bathing suit is tough to handle. A man with hunting clothes and boots would be an impossible task. And there was the bean field and mud to contend with."

"Where did he get the strength? I'm amazed at his effort. He seems to have done everything he could to save that guy."

"I think it will be difficult for the prosecutor to get a conviction because of Dean's heroic efforts."

After learning details of the accident, Karla was somewhat relieved. The facts tipped in Dean's favor. She still had a wait before she could see him, but she began to relax. She listened absentmindedly as the sheriff and attorney reflected on a scandal from back in the seventies.

The hospital where Dean was treated was named for Porter Rogers, Sr., a highly respected local doctor. His forty-year marriage ended with his wife's murder. Reportedly, he was in failing health and depended on an ambitious female employee as his *fountain of youth*. There was conjecture that he used her to hire her boyfriend to dispose of his wife. Dr. Rogers died sometime during the trial or appeal. Word at the time was that his employee/alleged lover and her boyfriend both went to maximum security units in Cummins Prison at Varner, near Gould.

Their talk was interrupted; an officer brought word that Karla could see Dean. She was escorted to a holding area. His face instantly told her that coming was the right decision. She held him close, and he poured out his grief. This was her man, and she was standing by him.

When the case reached the district prosecutor, he found no record on Dean Story, not even a ticket for speeding. The matter did not appear to be complex or difficult to handle. He assigned the case to his assistant and headed to the Bahamas for a vacation.

A couple weeks later, the deputy prosecutor arrived at his office, dumped his mail on his desk, and sat to enjoy his morning coffee. It was too hot, so he just sipped it and began to shuffle through the pile in front of him. There were a few documents and some personal bills that had come by U.S. Mail. He laid those aside to open a five-by-seven manila envelope without postage that had been dropped through the mail chute in his door.

Inside were fifteen one-hundred-dollar bills and a note of gratitude from Dean's father. The deputy prosecutor was preparing to move for dismissal when the money arrived. He put his conscience and the money in his wall safe, called the Bahamas, and left his boss a recorded message: "I decided to null pros the Story case. Thanks for your confidence in me. Have a nice vacation. Stay an extra week, if you like. See you when you return."

Dean's attorney had pocketed thirty-five hundred. Totaled, this was the least amount James Dean had paid out since Dean's fight at a high school homecoming dance.

Chapter 7

Though Arkansas Tech is a four-year school, Dean stayed only three and a half. After the accident on Dead Day, James Dean brought his son home. Dean had already grown into a big man, quickly recognized by his trademark Grizzly Adams beard—sprouted to celebrate Grayville's centennial.

With a neck two inches too large for any of his shirts, there were no ties in this man's wardrobe. Western clothing filled his closet. He wore jeans and cowboy boots. His belts had big buckles; and his nickname, Bull, was engraved on the back of each belt. For funerals, he wore black jeans, black shirt, black hat, black boots, and sometimes a black eye or two. He didn't like to fight; he was just active, assertive and accommodating.

He hired on at First Bank, working a teller window, posting checks, and even cleaning up after hours once when the janitor was ill. The bank was semi-computerized, and Dean knew more about computers than anyone on the staff. He never coasted on his father's position. He worked hard and earned the respect of all employees of the bank. He enjoyed working with his father and was a quick study. He was soon grounded in basics of the financial world and began to serve as the loan officer. The mix of his effort and personality brought the loan collection rate to ninety-five percent.

Dean was a gentleman always, poised and mannerly, and made friends wherever he went. Though he was a friend to all, he didn't have a best friend in Grayville. He was well known for three-day weekends out-of-town. He would meet one to five of probably a hundred buddies— many of whom would answer if you asked for "Bubba."

And, did they party! Word always seemed to find its way back to Grayville, except for the weekends he spent in Washington D.C. Then, there was nothing.

Dean was skilled at covering his tracks. But one event almost tripped him up. When Lawrence Suvenski opened an office in Paris, Texas, Dean asked if he could take that flight every Tuesday. On their first trip down and back, Dean surprised him saying, "Hey, let's stop for a few minutes in Mena. That's only five minutes out of your way, isn't it?" That evolved into a detour every time. The extra five thousand per week from his new office may have caused Lawrence to gloss over details. He never asked, "Why?" though he once overhead Dean talking on the phone about an exchange of tapes. They made fifteen round trips from Rogers, Arkansas, to Paris, Texas, by way of Mena.

On the day of the last one scheduled, the weather was challenging. Lawrence had never flown in such rough conditions. This thunderstorm, rising to fifty and sixty thousand feet, surpassed his rigorous training and seven missions in Desert Storm. A simulator had shown the windshield could handle the pounding of golf-ball-sized hail, but this was real life.

Lawrence saw concern on his passenger's face. "Hey, Dean, don't worry about this plane. We're taking a beating, but it's tough and powerful. We can pull out of about anything."

Suddenly, the plane nosed slightly forward, dropped about seven hundred feet, and continued falling. Dean cut him a worried look.

Lawrence tried to assure him. "Downdrafts sometimes come out of dense turbulent clouds. This probably means we have cleared the storm. We ought to be leveling off soon." He checked his gauges. "We're at 2300 and falling, 2200 . . . 2100 . . . ." He held tightly to the wheel, his knuckles turning white.

Dean bit his lip. "Shouldn't we be about to Mena?"

"I had to go around that big one at McAlister. We're coming in from the northwest instead of the southwest as we usually do. We need to hold our altitude at 2000 or get back up. We'll drift over Rich Mountain if this wind doesn't change directions. The last plane to crash on Rich Mountain went into the cliff side at 2173 feet. That mountain is over 1900 feet at the big end and some trees reach over 2200 at the peak. I'd rather be at 3000 to avoid trouble.

"You're kidding me, Lawrence. You mean we could hit that peak?"

"I hope not. In that last crash, fifty first-responders searched three days before finding the bodies. All aboard were killed, apparently on impact."

"You mean the plane didn't burn?"

"No. Pilots are trained to shut off their electrical supply."

Only a moment passed before both knew they were going down. Lawrence and Dean could no longer communicate. Inside the plane, nothing could be heard over the noise of vibrating and falling. Dean's mouth was moving and his head was shaking wildly. He couldn't hear Lawrence.

"I've got to hold back on the stick . . . keep the nose up . . . kill the switch . . . ."

The plane bounced off treetops and went airborne again. But damage to controls would not allow it to fly. The plane came down again, hit another tree, and turned sideways; then the wind caught it. Flipping over and rising again as if to pull out, the plane lost all momentum and came down on its tail. A rock on one side and three cedar trees on the other—like book ends—held it stationary. Lying one-hundred-fifty yards away, downhill about thirty feet, both pilot and passenger were unconscious.

When Dean came to, he cautiously moved his limbs. He could still function. His bruises were bone deep, but he had never given in to pain. He was first tagged *Bull* after gaining three-hundred-fifty yards rushing in an intramural championship football game his freshmen year at Tech—a record that stood for twenty-two years. Adrenaline, then party spirits, had held off pain until the day after. He faced that distance again, but this time carrying a rock-solid near-two-hundred-pound lump of life. Dean gathered Lawrence in his arms and headed from the crash site.

Ground fog gathered as the rain slowed, obscuring his vision. With eyes wide open to compensate, he steadily trudged forward. Distant lightning bathed the mountainside, intermittently illuminating his surroundings. A flash on the horizon caught his attention. "Yellow . . . ? What could it be?" He stopped and strained his eyes. He could see a flicker of faint light ahead. He thought, "No way!" There on a twenty-foot-wide flat area on the side of the mountain sat a school bus. Dean hoped their luck was taking a turn for the better. This far back in the woods, he could have stumbled onto criminals or illegal drug manufacturing. "Hey! Is anybody in there?"

Rich Mountain, one of the tallest points in the Midwest—
and Polk County's pride and joy, was frequented by three
sorts: vacationers and picnickers, public servants looking
for crash survivors, and fringe right-wingers. For the
latter, an old school bus made decent low-cost living
quarters. West of the mountain in La Flore County, Dean
had stumbled onto such a refuge.

The bus had been purchased just weeks before
at Wickes School's annual summer auction and cost six
hundred dollars. The night afterward, the owners' old
Volkswagen version was broken down and shoved into
brush beside Highway 71, south of Mena. There was no
registration, no way to trace the vehicle.

The bus family had connections to extremists over
the line in Oklahoma. They didn't live in the commune,
because the woman's half-black father disqualified them.
Pure white heritage was a strict requirement. But they
attended weekly rallies and no longer paid taxes.

In the bus, a young boy whimpered, "Mama, I'm scared. I
heard somebody hollering again."

"Everything's okay, honey, that's just the wind and
rain you're hearing." She had heard too and held him
tighter.

His father bristled. "Ya'll pipe down and stay back
here. I'll step out and see what the heck's going on."

"Hey! Is anybody there?" Dean was directing his
question to long double doors on the right side of the
bus, near the front.

Out of the dark came an answer. "Yo! Over here."
The mountain man had quietly exited the rear door. He

held a nine-millimeter semi-automatic in his right hand; in his left was a flashlight with a canister of pepper spray attached.

Dean inwardly recoiled from the gun, but he gripped Lawrence more tightly and slowly took a step forward. "We need help. Our plane crashed and my buddy passed out. He hasn't made a sound since the explosion."

"Lay your friend on the bench by my woodpile. I want a closer look."

The glare of the flashlight made Lawrence stir, and he quietly moaned as he was stretched on rough uneven boards.

"Tell me what you're doing here. What happened?"

"We were on our way to Paris, Texas. We went down in the storm. I lost consciousness too. I came to a distance from the plane. I checked the pilot and went back for a look at the wreckage. I needed to look for something in the back of the plane. I lit a propane burner so I could see. I accidentally dropped the burner. Realizing the danger, I took off running. The plane exploded as soon as I slid down that big rock and rolled over."

The man listened attentively, still eyeing Dean from a careful distance. He stood quietly a minute when he stopped talking, as if struggling with whether to believe what he had heard. He ordered, "Stay put."

He went inside and told his wife, "The noise we heard was a plane crash. There are two guys outside. The pilot may be hurt real bad. I'm going to drive them down the mountain." He came back out and readied their four-wheeler, which was outfitted with an extension on back for hauling his family. "Okay, load your friend here. I'm going to drive you to where you can get help."

Dean loaded Lawrence and climbed aboard beside him.

There are no phones atop Rich Mountain. When Dean and Lawrence were finally aboard an ambulance, there was no detouring. Karla had to wait.

In Waldron, he could have called had there been a phone. A *Bikers for Jesus* rally in the middle of the highway stalled traffic for ten minutes. Signs admonishing, *Love your neighbor as yourself* and *Jesus Only* were held high amid a contrasting collage of human, machine, and black leather. Drivers going both directions lined the road, some for the unique photo op, some just to gawk.

At Mansfield, the ambulance inched along the two-lane road for miles behind a flatbed load of shrink-wrapped Porta-Potties.

Three hours after leaving the mountain site, they reached St. Edward Mercy Hospital in Fort Smith. Lawrence was stabilized and quickly shuttled to ICU. Dean entertained the nurses and staff with stories while in the ER for treatment. He talked non-stop while waiting to visit Lawrence.

He was unforgettable. No one had difficulty giving details to the investigators. Dean's clothing smelled of fuel; the hair on his arms had the charred curl and stench of burning; and soot covered his backside. Lawrence, on the other hand, had injuries but no evidence of fuel or burn damage.

After Dean was checked and released, he headed to a phone. He was rewarded with Karla's soft "Hello".

"Karla, I'm so glad to hear your voice. You're always what I need when I'm down."

"What's the matter, Dean?"

"I'm at the ER at St. Edward in Fort Smith. I know I was supposed to call you last night, but we got delayed."

"My goodness, why are you at the ER, Dean?"

The story practically poured out. He told her about the storm, the crash, being thrown from the plane, and the pilot's injury. "When I came to, I remembered the Mena delivery, so I scrambled back up the mountain and took out the propane burner to use as a light. I was unable to reach the stuff and accidentally dropped the burner. As I ran back down the hill, I lost my footing. I was skidding down a rock when the plane exploded. I was partially hidden but was knocked down and sent rolling thirty feet. Somehow, I landed on my feet."

"Dean, it's a wonder you're still alive. Are you sure you're okay? I wish you wouldn't take chances like that."

"Hey, you heard me. Dean Story lands on his feet! I'm fine, and you're so fine. Come down and pick me up. I'm ready to get out of here."

Karla was on the road in minutes, made good time, and soon pulled in to claim her man. But they were hardly on their way when Dean spotted the truck stop at Alma and asked her to stop. He told her home-cooking was just what he needed. He glad-handed a few of the truckers and escorted Karla to a booth in the corner. He scanned the menu and bypassed the dinner entrees. The hour was so late that he opted for a country breakfast with coffee. Karla ordered a short stack, bacon, and apple juice.

Smoke hung in thick layers in the back, like fog on a cool morning. Karla was thankful it did not creep over to the booths; she hated smoke. Smoke was her family car that burned, her Dad puffing cigarettes, lung cancer, and clichés that haunted her the more she learned about Dean: "Where there's smoke, there's fire," "the smoking gun," and "We smoked 'em again, Bubba." The last one she had heard on double dates when Dean drag-raced to and from the movies.

Because of the hour, they didn't dawdle. They ate quickly and got back on the road. Not many miles later, Karla wished she'd had coffee. Dean was snoring. She grew sleepier by the minute. Finally, she realized the last miles would have wait until the next day. She had to sleep. She saw a *Vacancy* sign and pulled in. There was only one room available—two double beds; she checked them in. Despite his nickname, Dean sleepily trailed her to their room and crashed on the first bed, fully clothed. She pried his boots off. Then without even turning back her covers, she kicked off her flats, stretched with a weary sigh, and was out too.

The next morning, she knelt beside her bed as she had done since she was eight. "Lord, thank you for saving Dean and the pilot from the airplane crash. Please . . . ."

"I thank you, too, God. You know what? I think there was something supernatural in the way I survived the fall after that explosion. Was that you, God?"

Dean grew quiet, and Karla prayed awhile. After her "Amen," she hugged Dean, her eyes wet with joy. She saw the humble man he was deep down. "You don't know how to pray worth a hoot, Dean."

"Hey, I bet I got through!"

They laughed, and he grabbed her in a firm bear hug. They were rested and prayed up, ready to get home.

"How about getting breakfast to go, Karla?"

"You're driving. Let's do that."

A few miles from there, he spotted a drive-through. He pulled in and they ordered at the menu board. A quick pass by the cashier, and they were on the road again with breakfast burritos and coffee. They ate as he tooled toward home. Dean had his hands full managing his food and the steering wheel. He was quiet. She reflected on what he had said about the crash.

"Where did they take Lawrence, Dean?"

"He was transferred to Oklahoma City by helicopter."

"Why? He was already at a top trauma center."

"Lawrence required surgery. They told me his rare blood type wasn't readily available, and he needed extra precautions because of that."

Investigations of the crash turned up nothing concrete. The State Police and Polk County Sheriff stored their reports in a tickler file, to be revisited when the FAA made their findings known. The sheriff made a summary release to news media:

> Investigation of the recent Cessna 150 crash on Rich Mountain has tentatively concluded. Because the plane burned afterward, the contents, equipment, and controls left intact were insufficient for a definitive decision regarding cause of the crash. The FAA will release their findings later. Both the pilot, Lawrence Suvenski, and passenger, Dean Story, survived; the pilot remains hospitalized.

Three months later, the FAA sent out a mundane report; and the crash was forgotten—officially that is.

Kerri Watson spotted Dean's name in the press release about the plane crash on Rich Mountain. She had earlier recognized Dean in photos taken at the Mena Airport during the investigation of the Oliver North, Iran-Contra, and Mena connections. She thought, "What a coincidence." Like a bloodhound catching a fresh scent, she was reenergized.

She ran this new lead for details. She found nothing of significance in the files of the State Police. The Sheriff resisted when she asked to see his records, but she wasn't quitting. Armed with an FOI pamphlet and written request, she got him to relent.

Using a small workroom next to his file storage, Kerri pulled records and pored over them under the watchful eye of a possessive file clerk. The same clerk was *too busy* to help with the many files in disarray from previous searches. Kerri spent three long days without a lunch break. Then, *Bingo!* She found the Sheriff's report on the crash. She itemized his findings:

1) The plane, owned by Lawrence Suvenski, was fully insured.
2) There was no definitive evidence of mechanical failure.
3) The plane ended up on its tail, sandwiched between rocks and trees. Pilot Suvenski, and passenger, Dean Story, had been thrown clear, possibly on the second flip.
4) The passenger returned to the plane and lighted a propane torch to search for personal belongings (said belongings not specified).
5) The plane burned and was a total loss.
6) The ignition switch was found in the *off* position.
7) A torch was found in the cabin of the plane.
8) The explosion and fire that destroyed the plane were likely due to carelessness of the passenger.
9) The passenger had a blood alcohol level of .12 at the ER three hours after the crash.
10) The pilot was alcohol free.
11) The pilot suffered lacerations, a concussion, two broken ribs, and a dislocated left shoulder.
12) Hospital staff reported the passenger's clothing smelled strongly of fuel and was smeared with soot. The hair on his arms was charred.

A footnote indicated that an item of unidentifiable melted plastic was found wedged among the control cables of the flaps. Also of interest, at the hospital the pilot referred to regular Tuesday stop-offs at the Mena airport, which he presumed were for the passenger to make a tape switch. None of these was sufficient for probable cause.

Kerri made copies of the report then tried to stifle her smug satisfaction as she replaced the files and headed for the door.

Chapter 8

Arkansas Derby day, the last race of the season for Oaklawn Park in Hot Springs, promised to be a big day for Dean Story. He would be up at the crack of dawn, drive to Drake Field, board the American-Eagle commuter flight to Hot Springs, rent a car, and eat breakfast downtown in the beautiful spa city. That was his plan—not what took place.

The night before, he called Karla and told her about the trip. She was in her first year of teaching fourth grade at Root Elementary in Fayetteville. They telephoned each other regularly.

She asked, "So what are you wearing? You know I'll look for you if there's a report on the news."

"You wear red on Arkansas Derby day. Everyone will look alike. But I'll smile really big just for you."

"Be careful, Dean."

"Hey, everything's fine. I'm . . . ."

"I know. I know. You're fine and I'm so fine. Just be sure you don't mess up down there and get fined!"

His morning alarm didn't go off. Next, he was already dressed in new jeans and a bright red *Hog* shirt when he discovered a flat on his Cherokee. He mounted the spare, put the flat in the rear, washed his hands, and dusted his boots on his pant leg. The engine wouldn't hit a lick. He opened the rear door again.

"Jumper cables! Where are the darn things? I only have forty minutes before the plane leaves. Where did I put those cables?" He headed for the storage room. The phone rang.

His mother could see his place from her kitchen window. "Are you going to Hot Springs today, or not?"

That was all he needed, a reminder. He was trying; this was just not his day. "Yes, Mom, I'm going. I overslept, had a flat, and now the Cherokee battery is dead. Suppose somebody's trying to tell me something? Mom, could you drive over and give me a boost?"

"Sure. Just give me a minute to change out of my robe."

He found the cables and was ready when she arrived. He got the engine running and was off. Five minutes in the opposite direction from Drake Field, he shook his head. He had headed to work absent-mindedly. He was not on the way to the airport. His watch showed seven-forty-five; the plane would leave at eight-eleven. He had to hurry.

Down the road he was stopped. He moaned, "Wouldn't you know it?" Garz Shouppe, the great grandpa of the Shouppe cattle operation, was moving cattle from one side of his place to the other.

In 1941, Arkansas joined with the federal government to construct a fourteen mile section of *hard road*—so called by home folks—between the Oklahoma line and Highway 62 in western Washington County and northern Gray Springs County. The new road split Shouppe's thirteen thousand acres in two.

The Land Grant Act following Reconstruction set aside the sixteenth section of all townships in Arkansas counties for a school. Some are still owned by the county education office. Prior to the 1930's there was an eight-grade one-room school on Shouppe's land. When this school consolidated with the other twenty-two county school districts, he bid and bought the section. When he later parceled out the farm to second-generation families, he kept the divided sixteenth section with the old school house.

Dean waited eight minutes for the cattle to pass. That was a record; the crossing animals once took fifteen. Shouppe never seemed to worry about traffic. The first time a state trooper confronted him about moving two to four hundred head of cattle across a US/State highway, he was ready with a comeback.

"Drivers got eyes; let them use 'em. And them cars have brakes, too. I start at seven forty-five in the morning and get done by a little after eight. Commuters are long gone by then if they care anything about their jobs. The others will just have to wait. I been doing this since 1953, and I ain't stoppin' now. Just write me a ticket and get along. I ain't gonna stand around long waiting."

The trooper reminded him to use safety flaggers, thanked him for his time, and left. And that was that. Troopers came and went. Shouppe never changed.

Dean missed the plane. He had to figure something out. When he spotted a phone, he stopped and called the Springdale flight service station. He connected with a plane preparing to depart for Hot Springs. In minutes, he had arranged a ride with three businessmen from Rogers. The pilot was his old friend, Bubba.

"Yeah, Dean, come on up. We'll wait for you. This is an eight-passenger baby, and we only have three going. Hey, you haven't been dieting, have you?"

"What are you talking about, Bubba? You know me."

"Then with you we'll be full."

Dean laughed. He could dish it out, too. "Watch your mouth. I'll sit on you." The day was shaping up to be interesting. He took Crossover Road, a north-south artery on the eastern edge of Fayetteville, and reached the Springdale Airport in twelve minutes. He grabbed his things and jogged to the plane. He opened the door and climbed into the right rear seat.

"Okay, let's get on it, Bubba! Man, I'm glad to see you. That goes for you, too, Dubba Bubba. It's been too long. I can't believe how this is working out. What's it been, three or four years since we've been together? Hot Springs better look out. We'll bust it wide open." He reached to shake hands with the passenger to his left. "Hello, Padna. If you're willing to go with these guys, I guess you can handle me. I'm not much worse. So, Dubba Bubba, what are you guys doing nowadays?"

"We're working together doing consultant work in Springdale. We work with businesses on recycling to improve the environment. We have an office in Lowell. What about you? Did you land at the bank with your dad?"

"Yes. And I enjoy working with him. We've turned out to be a pretty good team. He's easy going. I've learned a lot from him. What about Padna, back here?"

"I'm sorry, Dean. I should have already introduced you. But I know you'll never get past calling him Padna, so let's leave it at that."

"Actually, I've met Padna. I get around, you know. But we've never spent much time together." He had met Rodgers Eugene Arnold two years before at a planning session for Renaissance Renewal Weekend. Within twenty-four hours, he had dubbed him *Padna*, and the name stuck. "Where did you two meet him?"

"We met in Eureka Springs at a little gambling venue. Bubba and I still enjoy placing a few bets. That's why we're headed to Hot Springs. We want a piece of the action at Oaklawn. Bubba tells us you're also going to the race track."

"Yes. But I want breakfast first. Have you guys eaten?"

Bubba was quick to reply. "Dubba Bubba and I haven't even had our coffee this morning. We're with you."

"What about you, Padna? Could you handle a morning spread?"

"I'm primed for breakfast. Just point me in the right direction."

"Well, I'm buying all of you the best; and I'll chauffeur you around if I can get a van or big car. Without this flight I'd probably have headed back home and missed everything."

Bubba said, "Our pleasure, Dean. I'm glad it worked out this way. We're over Mt. Magazine now, and we should be in the restaurant eating within forty-five minutes.

Once you rent a vehicle, a fifteen minute drive will get us to downtown Hot Springs; and we can all pig out."

"Hey, fine landing, Bubba. I thought the wind would give you more trouble. When the left wing dipped at the last minute and you touched down on that left wheel, I figured you would have to wrestle the thing down. How'd you make it so smooth?"

"I just dropped the flaps, reversed thrust and held her on the horizon. The plane did the rest."

After locking the plane down, they walked over to the car rental desk. "I'm sorry. We've had a sell-out today. All I have left are two specialty items: First, a 1955 Chevy truck used by an ice cream vendor. The top was chopped off and replaced with snapped-on canvas. This jewel is two-tone pink with fender-skirts and four bucket seats. The refrigeration is gone, but the ice cream compartments are there. Think of all that space for luggage."

"I think I'll pass. What else you got?"

"The other vehicle is a Humvee, but it rents for seventy-five dollars a day."

"I'll take it. Here's my card."

He completed the rental before someone could beat him to it. The other clerk was engaged with four thirty-something macho types, and Dean feared he was about to rent the Humvee. He didn't know they all worked for the rental agency.

"All right, a Razorback red Humvee!" Bubba exclaimed. He asked to drive, but Dean wouldn't hear of it.

"I'm the designated driver of this baby. You guys just load 'er up, and we'll get this hog on the road."

The weather was beautiful, and there was a record crowd. At eight o'clock that morning, the streets had filled with pre-race motoring to dine, antique hunt, sight-see, and shop. The traffic had only worsened. For those in the Humvee, the forty-five minutes until *pig out* had expired. They still had a fifteen-minute ride to breakfast at *Centre Mall*. Traffic was slow at first, then stalled. There was a 4x4 GMC in the next lane. Dean lowered his window.

"What's going on up ahead?"

"A minute ago, I heard a report on the radio about a bad fire in a restaurant at *Centre Mall*. Two employees were taken away by ambulance. The fire department has the road blocked off. That end of the mall is temporarily closed."

Dean came unglued. This was too much. His arms beat the air. They beat the steering wheel. He ranted. "This is not my lucky day, boys! No alarm, a flat tire, a dead battery, a missed plane, no rental cars or vans, and now no food! No food! I'm not sure I even need to show up at Oaklawn. I'll probably lose my shirt." Foreign he was not, but Dean's animation mimicked a ticked-off Italian. The time was nine-twenty-five; just thirty-five minutes remained until post time for the first of ten big races on the last day of the Oaklawn season.

At nine-fifty, cars were frantically vying for openings in the lanes ahead. With horns blowing, most of the drivers were single-mindedly focused on Oaklawn. Dean swerved quickly into a drive-through. He ordered, "Two sausage biscuits with egg, a large orange juice and black coffee."

"Make that two," came from the back. "Make it three," from his right, and a rear-seat "Four" made things simple.

The microphone answered, "That will be eighteen dollars. Pull around to the first window, please."

Bubba said, "Food, fellas, food!" as sacks were passed. "Now let's get over there, grab us a racing form and program, get our bets down, and win some money."

Dean garbled, "We're on our way." His mouth was full as he reentered traffic. They all virtually inhaled their breakfast as the Humvee inched forward. None seemed fazed to have just minutes before the start of the race when they entered the parking lot. They hoofed it inside and placed bets.

"They're off for the lead. Bay Side Stride is first on the inside, followed by Treacherous, then Fargo, Bright Boy, and Little John."

Bubba had twenty on Fargo to win, place, or show. Dubba Bubba placed twenty on Old Gray Mare to win. Dean had the longshot, Juco, faded with five hundred to place or show; and Padna bet ten on Bay Side Stride.

"Up on the outside Old Gray Mare has taken second behind the leader, Bay Side Stride. Third is Treacherous, followed by Fargo, Bright Boy, Little John, and the pack. Back of the pack, in last place, running on the outside, is Juco."

Dean knew Juco held back, but he thought, "This is ridiculous. Why would a horse run the outside when in last place? My handicapper's tip must have been wrong."

"Juco is due, Bull; he is due. He will love this race. This long one is his, baby. He closes fast on the last three furlongs, and the longer he runs the faster he gets. Put a fiver on him to place or show. No way can he beat Bay Side Stride, 'cuz the Stride has endurance and sprint speed. He's never been beat if he's leadin' at the two-furlong mark."

Dean had given the handicapper a hundred dollars and placed the bets just as recommended. They were a good team. The handicapper said so. "You've got the money, buddy; I've got the time." Dean was happy to be in business with this genius. Over the past six years, he was ahead six thousand after expenses on races handicapped by this guy.

"Bay Side Stride is in the lead in the back stretch. Old Gray Mare is second, Fargo third, Bright Boy fourth, and on the inside Juco is closing fast on the leaders. With three furlongs to go, it's Bay Side Stride, Old Gray Mare and Juco. Boy! Juco is moving! The race is between those three. The pack is six lengths behind and fading."

Dean was on his feet. "Come on, Juco! Atta boy! Come on home, baby. Keep it up! Pour it on!" The horse must have heard him. At that point, Juco sprinted past numbers three, two and one to finish first—five lengths ahead of Bay Side Stride and Fargo.

The crowd was up out of their seats, jumping up and down, yelling, and cheering—each one in direct proportion to the success of their wagers. Dean was grinning from ear to ear. He said, "Fifty to one. That's great!" His take was twenty thousand on Juco and another three hundred on Bay Side Stride, who finished second and paid six to one. The State had gotten its twenty-five percent up front. Bubba won thirty dollars on Fargo. Bay Side Stride won Padna sixty dollars.

Dubba Bubba lost his twenty but seemed to feel good anyway. "I wouldn't take anything for that race. You don't see shows like that anywhere else but Hollywood. Besides, I can still bet on the rest of them."

One down, nine to go. Dean had his pencil out marking the form with bets on the other races. He planned to bet five hundred on each of the handicapper's picks in the next eight races and up it to twenty-three hundred on the Arkansas Derby. He figured that if he lost every race the rest of the day, he would still take twelve thousand eight hundred away. If he won one or two more, he could handle that too.

After six more wins, Dean's billfold was bulging. His win on the Arkansas Derby was anticlimactic. His high came from the first race. He left with twenty six thousand seven hundred dollars. Bubba broke even after expenses; Dubba Bubba came out a hundred over. Padna hit the last three and the daily double, taking home a thousand. None of his wins came on a long shot, none from a tip; he was a thinker. The crowd was thinning as Dean and his crew moved toward the exit. He asked, "Anybody hungry?"

Dubba Bubba exaggerated, "I could eat a horse." Then he laughed; his quip fit the day.

Bubba laughed too and said, "So could I. Who's buying?"

Dean said, "Everything's on me again, team. What'll it be?" He felt generous. He was toting big bucks!

Padna added, "I'll get the drinks and appetizers."

Dean did and Padna did. When every morsel was gone, the group loaded up and headed for the airport.

Back at the car rental desk, Dean made an offer for the Humvee. He had cash and ideas for the *Hog*, as he called it.

"Sorry, it's not for sale. I can rent it to you by the month for a good price, though."

"What's the deal?"

"It'll run you a thousand a month, but you get free miles. Charge it on your card a month at a time. If you return with a month incomplete, you get the unused days credited back to you."

He wanted the Hog. "I'll take it for a month. Here's my card. Set it up while I see my friends off." He walked to the plane. Bubba was beginning flight procedures inside. He had completed the preflight walk-around, and engines would soon be fired. Dean opened the side door and stuck his head in. "Thanks again guys for good company, all the fun, and the ride down. That Humvee and I are headed to Louisiana Downs."

Padna was stretched out, seatbelt locked in place, his head lain back on a rolled up inflatable raft. His feet were propped up on what looked like a parachute. He looked ready. Dean saluted him and said, "Padna, I can tell by looking at you. Everything's fine." He stepped out and went down the exit singing, "Steppin' on the clouds,

we'll see Jesus. Rise to meet Him in the air. Steppin'
on the clouds, He will greet us. Oh, the joy, together,
we will share. He's gonna leave this world behind him,
going where the devil cannot find him." The old spiritual
seemed to fit the occasion.

Chapter 9

As Dean claimed his "Hog", the Lear Jet ascended, leveling off at four thousand feet, eight miles north of Hot Springs. Bubba banked westward and set the controls to bring the plane down gently into Lake Ouachita. According to their map, cruising at a hundred-fifty miles per hour with very little wind, the plane would hit the water about six miles northwest of the airport. Dubba Bubba opened the right hand door and jumped; Bubba followed out the left. They fell about a thousand feet before deploying their chutes, to give the plane time to be out of line of sight—lessening the chance someone would spot them coming down. Right on course, the plane descended below the mountain peak and out of view. Only about fifteen gallons of fuel remained when they jumped; there would be no explosion.

The sky was clear, the weather warm and humid; hardly anyone was on the lake. Two fishermen watched the plane from their boat in the shade.

"I believe that plane's gonna try to land on the lake."

"Looks like something fell off the plane. Did you see that?"

"Yeah, I did. Didn't that look like a parachute? They may be in trouble."

"Or, that could be a stunt pilot and a skydiver. You can see anything around here on Arkansas Derby day." He watched as the plane eased toward the water, tail touching first, then the belly. "Boy, that guy can sho' nuff land a plane."

The plane began to sink.

"Hey, that plane's going under. We'd better get help. The pilot may be sick or hurt."

The fishermen motored to the closest pier and ran to borrow a phone. Word quickly spread after the 911 call, and a crowd gathered on the bank near the pier. The sheriff's deputy arrived in a few minutes and asked the fisherman who had phoned, "Did the pilot get out of the plane before it sank?"

"My buddy and I saw someone parachute out of the plane back toward the ridge on the north side."

A woman standing nearby broke in, "I thought I saw two parachutes back there over the ridge." She had been in her back yard up the road when the sound of the plane's descent caught her attention. Trying to fix her eyes on the plane, she had spotted two parachutes. Over the next hour, these stories were repeated several times by others. The deputy concluded that some had seen both parachutes, and others had seen only one of the two.

One of his assistants called him aside. "We have no new leads on the plane crash or the survivors. Looks like those guys dropped out of the sky and out of sight. There's not a trace of them anywhere. We've been all over, down all the roads and cut-offs."

"Well, you boys go over to the convenience store at the intersection of Highways 7 and 298 and check out that stolen car report. I'll stay on this for a while. The owner of the car called thirty minutes ago."

The deputy headed out to question lake-shore residents. He asked one after another, "Did you folks see any parachutes out north of the lake this afternoon about five fifteen?"

Only one had a report. "The only thing I saw all afternoon was that big green helicopter—could have been Army or Air Force. They seemed to be looking for something. Maybe the plane, maybe drugs. The thing went over, wasn't gone more than ten minutes—if that long, and flew back."

The deputy had lost the trail. His strategy didn't include chasing a helicopter. He turned his attention to other cases. He reported, "Two bailed out north of the ridge before the plane hit the water." The news media honed in on that as fact, and the issue was not pursued. The wire service sent out the story, which surfaced as small back-page filler in local and regional newspapers across the country:

> Lear Jet Crashes in Lake Ouachita.
> Two Parachute to Safety. One Missing.
>
> Hot Springs, Arkansas. An eight-passenger Lear jet crash-landed Saturday into Lake Ouachita, six miles northwest of the city. Fishermen saw it hit the water. They reported a parachute descending in the area. Two passengers are believed to have parachuted from the plane north of the lake over the ridge area. An airport spokesperson said a third person was aboard the flight; none of the three has been seen since. The pilot failed to file a flight plan. The FAA has authorized reclamation of the wreckage. An investigation is under way. Results will be forthcoming.

While the deputy ran his investigation, Bubba and Dubba Bubba had been digging nearby in a wooded area. They quickly buried their chutes and clothing. Bubba said, "A little more sand and pine straw ought to do it." They hid every trace of their handiwork. Wearing just shorts and T-shirts, they jogged east on Arkansas 298 toward Jessieville, looking for a vehicle to use.

"This is it!" Dubba Bubba had spotted keys dangling from the ignition of a brand new Saturn outside a liquor store, with no driver in sight. Ten seconds later, they were in the car and rolling out of Jessieville on Highway 7. Passing by Hot Springs Village, they made tracks for Morrilton and I-40 west.

Bubba had been scanning the road ahead for a convenience store. He saw one coming up. "Hey, pull in and go get us some drinks and snacks. Drop something glass, fumble around apologizing, and attempt to clean it up. While they're distracted, I'll pull us a set of plates. We've gotta switch these out to get past Mountainburg. Cars have to crawl through that town. If the cops are on to us, they will definitely be checking tags. And we'll be going so slow, they can't miss us."

Dubba Bubba pulled in; they left with tags and refreshments, their heads held high. At Alma, they turned north on Scenic Highway 71. Bubba mounted the tags at the Rudy exit using a quarter as a screwdriver. He bragged, "Not bad, two minutes thirty seconds."

"What's our number?"

"PAID-4. Funny, isn't it? We steal a car and tag it *paid for.* Yeah, and we got paid to do so. We couldn't have done better. Someone lost an expensive plane, but we kept their butts out of prison."

"When they find the plane, won't the FAA or the law find out who owned it?"

"There's no way. There was no identification of any kind on or in the plane—no flight plan and no finger prints. That's why we wore those gloves and why we kept the cockpit closed. Dean's hands were all over, and that could mean trouble for him. We squeaked by on the flight plan. But I figured, with all those planes coming in, Hot Springs couldn't keep up with half of them; and we'd be in the half they missed."

They drove late into the night to distance themselves from the plane crash. They had brought an end to Padna and his investigation. There were no strings attached. They could focus on spending their pay.

Dean was involved from the beginning, but he would draw little suspicion on this one. When the plane crashed, he and the Humvee were already out of town; he reached Arkadelphia before the deputy finished his questioning. He stopped for coffee at a drive-in. Noticing a phone outside, he decided to call Karla. As he lifted the receiver, men nearby were talking about the crash. He hesitated momentarily to listen.

"I heard on the radio that they found the plane but no bodies. Witnesses saw two parachutes descend, but they haven't found them yet." Dean's coins clanged down the slot, and he quickly dialed.

"Hello."

"Karla, I'm down at Arkadelphia, and I . . . ."

"Oh, Dean, you're not in jail are you?"

"Heck no! I cleaned up at Oaklawn, and I'm on my way to Louisiana Downs."

"So, what are you driving? Your Mom mentioned you were having trouble with your Jeep this morning."

"I left it at the airport in Springdale. I caught a ride with Bubba and Dubba Bubba. Remember them? I couldn't believe such good luck after my rotten start. We had a great time. Anyway, I rented a Razorback-red Humvee—my very own Hog! I'm making it just fine."

"Well, be careful, Dean. I love you."

"Back at you. I'll call when I get to Bossier." Coffee in hand, Dean boarded the Hog and drove off. Padna was history.

Padna grew up in Kansas. From an early age, he was interested in aerodynamics. While still a youth, he experienced his first hot-air balloon ride, rode in a crop-duster, and helped his uncle build an experimental plane. Actually, he admitted later, it was a gyrocopter. But his most unique memory was watching a plane fly backward down a valley—possible because of thirty-mile-per-hour winds that prevailed for hours in the aftermath of a hurricane.

He attended Kansas State on a Merit Scholarship, majoring in electrical engineering. Two semesters he was in the cooperative program as a trainee at the McDonald-Douglas plant in the Saint Louis metro area. His job was electronic security for computer systems and perimeter observation analyses. He focused on trouble-shooting software, performance data, production and cost analyses, and abnormal personnel behavior. He attempted software invasions, background-checked employees working in critical areas, and exhaustively tried to infiltrate the security systems.

His superior asked him to investigate a suspected breach of security tied to more than a million dollars in computer chip over-purchases and losses. In the process, he uncovered an apparent conspiracy between a middle manager and a labor leader to commit fraud. Losses in radar and in-flight control components were trailed to their desks. By panning background data, he learned these two had worked in other companies with huge inventory losses in the same areas. He suspected they were selling to foreign governments or the underworld of Europe or Asia. Their phone and e-mail records yielded evidence for all three.

How his tentative report got into other hands he would never know. Before the matter was publicized, voice messages at his office warned him to stop his investigation immediately, or he would be killed. A written warning—newsprint letters pasted on his superior's letterhead—came by interoffice mail. He could take no obvious action, and certainly not at his office. He wasn't sure who was involved. He decided to leave town. To avoid being tailed, he zigzagged his way to St. Charles.

First, he took a cab to Riverfront Mall and eased into a group sight-seeing in the Arch. He blended in as they walked out and westward toward the *beer gardens.* He ducked into a restroom; and, when the next cluster of tourists passed, he slipped out to join them. He stopped at a gift shop and bought a souvenir Busch Gardens hat, a St. Louis Cardinals baseball cap, and two T-shirts. At the next restroom, he changed his Oxford shirt for one of the T-shirts and switched his sun visor with the hat. He stowed his things in the shopping bag from the gift shop. He rolled his pants legs up and shed his socks, then briefly checked the *tourist* looking back from the mirror. He fit the mold.

Four more diversions convinced him he wasn't being followed, so he hopped a bus. He phoned his superior from the bus station in St. Charles. He explained his need for evasive action and gave his location. He told him to check the inter-office mail; his research was there in the form of a routine status report.

Twenty minutes later, a driver arrived with a charge card, credentials, overnight articles, and passage to Fayetteville, Arkansas. The driver was an armed security expert and stayed with him until he registered at the Inn at the Mill in Johnson, on the north edge of Fayetteville. He would lay low there while preparations were made. His superior was lining up a job for him as an adjunct professor in engineering at the University of Arkansas until after his testimony in court.

Bubba and Dubba Bubba were hired by the accused McDonald-Douglas employees to get rid of Padna. First they had to shake him out of the bushes. He was known to gamble—"no preference, just any game of chance." They scheduled *Vegas Casino* events—gambling fronted with play money—in six populous areas within seven hours of St. Louis. When they publicized the dates, Padna foolishly responded. After contact was established, the remaining *Vegas Casino* evenings were cancelled.

He attended the one in Eureka Springs, Arkansas. Throughout the evening, they moved in on him. They told him they were in Springdale doing consultant work on recycling to improve the environment. They had set up a dummy office in nearby Lowell where they easily blended in because of the steady influx of new employees for the headquarters of Tyson, J.B. Hunt Trucking Company, and Walmart. Before the night's end, they had set up the trip to Oaklawn Park. They would fly to Hot Springs for a day of horseracing; on the way back, the *accident* would happen. The day of their trip to Oaklawn, Dean called and wanted to join them. Bubba let him ride. He could take the fall for them. Isn't that what friends are for?

Chapter 10

Booking it down the road in his Hog, Dean arrived in Texarkana about seven that evening. Going left on Highway 71, he came to College Hill and a sign that read, *Hobo Jungle Park*. He had heard stories about the place.

In Texarkana in the 1930's, Cotton Belt Railroad's switching yard divided the *haves* and *have-nots*. The label, *north of the railroad,* meant affluence. Men out of work during the Dust Bowl and the Depression hitched rides to search for work. When trains stopped to switch, load, and unload in Texarkana, these men without means were forced to layover at Hobo Jungle. Empty boxcars which were parked along spur lines south of the railroad became temporary quarters on the sly for two or three and sometimes up to thirty hobos.

Dreams shared around the campfire built camaraderie and kept hope alive. A three-gallon cast-iron pot hung over the fire continually—never washed, always hot with stew for the hungry. Hobos added to and took out as needed; once a stew lasted more than sixteen months. Protein was primarily what could be caught—squirrel, raccoon, chicken, dove, quail, and rabbit. Vegetables were scavenged from gardens or donated from knapsacks of new arrivals. The public well beside the old College Hill Post Office held water for anyone willing to prime the pump.

Dean's mind wandered until he had driven completely out of town, away from fast food and restaurants. Evening was becoming dark night, and he was starved. About fifteen miles south of Texarkana on Highway 71, he reached a diner still open in Fouke, Arkansas. He wheeled in.

Ron Austin

The waitress saw him come through the door and smiled. "Good evening. Would you prefer a table or a booth?"

Dean chose a table in the middle of the room. He ordered the special of the day—chicken-fried steak with creamed potatoes and gravy, fried okra, corn on-the-cob, and cornbread—with a large tea and lemon.

His tea came in a quart jar with a handle, adorned with four lemon wedges and a huge wooden stir stick. He chuckled. The waitress told him she discovered chopsticks among supplies bought at auction from a Chinese restaurant. They didn't exactly fit the diner, but she had found a use for them. As Dean doctored his tea, excited voices drew his attention to teenagers in the corner booth.

"Did you hear about the principal nailing the seniors this morning?"

Curiosity kept him focused as the details poured out. Two of them had been in the hall at eleven-forty-five that morning and heard the principal lambast the seniors in a hastily called class meeting. That meeting lasted until five after twelve. The seniors missed their eleven-fifty lunch privilege and had to line up behind the younger classes, who went at noon.

Dean caught their names—Terry, Kenny and Larry Wayne—and managed to figure out who was who. He pieced together that these guys were juniors who had gotten one on the seniors.

The door opened, and another teen walked in. "You guys hear about the seniors getting crawled today? They are some kind of mad! What was that all about?"

This was brag time. Kenny said, "We climbed in the school through a window last night. We toilet-papered the place, wrote *Seniors 1983* with white shoe polish on the mirrors and door glass, shave-creamed the lockers, and put Vaseline and KY Jelly on the door knobs, toilet seats and pencil-sharpener handles. We turned student desks upside down, and switched all the teachers' middle desk drawers. And last, we hoisted the business teacher's desk to the roof of the main high school building."

The newcomer said, "Wow! "How'd you get in the rooms?"

Terry replied, "We got a key from the custodial supervisor. We told him we had a class project that was running late, and we needed to lock up. He believed us, always does." They all had a real laugh.

The custodian had twenty-eight years on the job, he had seen it all. He just played along. When the school principal told him about the incident, he replied, "What'll they think of next? They sure made a mess. They ought to have to clean it up." The principal made sure of that. He kept the seniors after school. Several protested innocence, but not too strongly; there was a chance classmates were guilty and hadn't owned up. Most of them were proud of their class accomplishment and walked around with a cocky attitude for weeks.

Dean had finished his meal and moved his chair to the corner where they were. "Hey, guys. My name is Dean Story. Sounds like you boys are slick. Do you think you will get caught?"

"No, never," Terry told him. "Just like they didn't find out we're the ones who made monster tracks on the playground last year at Halloween."

Dean said, "Monster tracks . . . ." His wheels were turning. "*The Legend of Boggy Creek* was about the Fouke monster, wasn't it?" This lit a fire under them. They all tried to talk at once. In just minutes, he realized he could have a little fun while these boys helped with his next agenda item. "That's why I'm in the area—to take the monster captive for relocation to its native Australia."

The boys took the bait. They had a reputation in their little town for pulling pranks. Dean looked like he was fair pickings for a few laughs. Terry kicked things off. "Larry Wayne, you saw it last, didn't you?"

"Yeah, but, I didn't think nothing of it at the time. That thing shows up with the full moon regular as clockwork down where the creek hits Sulfur River. I've seen it seven times in the last eight months. I figured it was sick in January—never did see it. We have plaster casts of the tracks. They must be nineteen to twenty inches long and eight to ten inches wide, and there's a knot on one toe. Would you like to see them?"

These Fouke High juniors were good. Dean was better. He thought, "This is great. They will think I'm the butt of the joke." He answered, "No, I believe you. But you guys could help me. I'm on my way to Louisiana Downs for some vacation time. When I come back, how about taking me to the area where the monster has been sighted?" He made plans with them for the following weekend.

As Fouke's pranksters set their trap, Dean was developing his own scenario. He knew Taylor Nicholas, a San Antonio savings and loan executive who had blown the whistle on a Texas State Senator for fraudulent land deals. The senator had been found guilty, fined a million dollars, and permanently barred from holding a securities license. After the trial, he vowed publicly to make Taylor pay. The Bureau of Domestic Intelligence agent in San Antonio received concrete evidence of a contract on Taylor's life.

Dean figured the senator's threat gave Taylor cause to get out of town. Dean decided to use Taylor to teach a lesson to Fouke's jokesters. In the process, he could keep an eye on Taylor a day or two while plans were finalized.

Taylor took a leave of absence. He arrived in Shreveport with a new clean-shaven look, dyed hair, and looser fitting clothing. He met Dean at Monica's Place, a little out-of-the way cafe located two blocks from LSU Medical Center. Patronized almost exclusively by doctors, nurses, techs, staff, and patients' families, the restaurant was a well-chosen meeting place. Taylor entered using a walker and wearing a hospital bracelet. After their meal together, he left with Dean in the red Humvee.

Kenny, Terry, and Larry Wayne met the bus that passed through Fouke overnight en route to Lake Charles, Louisiana. They were there to pick up the gorilla suit rented from Helene's in Fort Smith. Larry Wayne grabbed the package and shoved it toward Terry. "Terry, you do this outfit justice!"

Kenny kidded, "Definitely an improvement in his looks. So, hey, what's our plan?"

They were all familiar with the Sulfur River landing west of Highway 71. Terry said that they would meet south of the bridge at the storage shed up the gravel road from there. He would suit up at seven-thirty in the morning and ride a mule down to the sixty-acre bean field that lay between the highway and the river. The mule would be tied to a tree on the bank, close enough to drink; and they would leave oats to keep it satisfied. Larry Wayne would handle the sound system. At appropriate times, he would release intermittent monster sounds. Terry would move around, jumping up here and there for Dean to see, running twenty yards or so then dropping down again between the five-foot-high bean rows. Kenny would be Dean's guide and make sure he spotted Terry.

The next day, however, Dean and Taylor showed up an hour and a half earlier than the boys. During the night, one of Dean's contacts had air-lifted an eight-foot-tall Big Foot suit from Hollywood to an oilfield along the Red River. Dean retrieved it; Taylor would be the Fouke monster.

The realistic state-of-the-art costume had been used in two domestic films and one foreign movie. The feet were slightly larger than those the boys described to Dean; they were inside-adjustable to fit the wearer. The suit's double-layered two-ply skin filled with gelatin provided cushion for falls and blows, was virtually tear proof, and was impenetrable by normal rifle or pistol bullets. A steel-capped bullet could penetrate one layer and inflict a harsh bruise but would not go through both two-ply layers. The head fit like a football helmet and had holes for eyes, ears, and mouth. A four-foot-long sipping tube was clipped near the mouth and connected to a quart flask held in a midsection pocket. Drop-down Velcro flaps provided plumbing.

Taylor found a large fallen tree and sat on it
in the cool shade while waiting for his curtain call.
Temperatures had been in the mid-thirties during the
night; the morning began cool and cloudy, clearing as the
sun came up. When Terry arrived, he crouched in the
direct sun. His gorilla suit was soon sweltering inside,
even though the temperature had barely reached forty-
five degrees. For both, a fifteen-minute wait ended with
sounds of chatter, footsteps, and the snap of brittle bean
stalks from last year's crop.

Kenny had escorted Dean across the bridge and
along the road which led to the field and boat-loading
ramp. Kenny stopped and listened. Down the bean rows
and over several yards, Larry Wayne had the sound
cranked up. Dean heard, but he didn't let on at first,
allowing Larry Wayne full range to create the effect they
had planned. He had the sounds just right to make one's
skin crawl. "Aarrrghh, Aarrrghh. Wheeeeeeooooiiieee.
Aarrghh, Wonkkh, Wonkkh. Wooieee Aarrrghh!"

Dean pretended alarm. "Kenny, that sounds like a
gorilla. You don't think the Boggy Creek Monster could
actually be a gorilla, do you?"

This opened the door for Kenny to trigger his plan.
"I don't know, could be. I've never actually seen him. The
way everyone describes him, I'd say he must be at least
eight feet tall. Maybe he is a gorilla." He was weaving
his way through the rows of stalks to set Dean up for a
sighting.

Seeing the tops of their heads, Terry leaped up,
waving both gorilla arms over his head in slow-motion as
if they weighed a ton. He then ran about fifty feet down
a bean row away from Dean and Kenny and dropped down
out of sight. He turned right and scampered below the
bean tops out of view toward the woods. Still ducking

below the stalks, he made his way another fifty yards then leaped up again, flailing his arms as before.

Larry Wayne was struggling to keep up while holding the tape player in the right direction and trying to stay out of sight.

Terry was doing a good job giving just a peek now and then. Dean saw Terry both times but waited for Kenny to announce the sightings. Kenny moved in closer, so they could spring the monster on Dean big time. He signaled with his clicker three times, paused for a five count and repeated—*Click, click, click*, and again, *click, click, click*. This told Terry to hold still for sixty seconds and make another appearance. Dean was sure to see him the next time.

Dean reached into his backpack and pulled out a tranquilizer dart-gun. He popped the shoulder bar in place, locked it, and raised the sights. Kenny's eyes grew big as saucers, and he nearly choked trying to speak. He couldn't get a word out.

"One shot's all I get," Dean said, trying to focus. "I have to make this count."

Kenny finally yelped, "Dart-gun! Who you gonna shoot?"

Dean calmly replied, "I have to tranquilize the monster for transport. He's headed for the Outback. How did you think I would take him?"

"I . . . I . . . I'm not sure I thought about it. Does that thing do permanent damage?" His hand shook so that he could hardly fumble the clicker out of his pocket. He quickly sounded a new signal, *Click,*

click, click, click, followed by a burst from his whistle, *Whizzzzzzzzzzzzzzzzz.*

This told Terry to count to forty then run like crazy to the woods and hide. Terry never saw the dart gun. He simply followed Kenny's signal, running wide open toward the dense brush ahead.

Anticipating the boys' reaction to the dart-gun, Dean had activated the lapel microphone of his tiny FM radio transmitter. A receiver clipped to Taylor's ear picked up the conversation: "Kenny, he's heading for the woods. I'm gonna move into better position so I can get a good shot." Dean broke into a trot down the bean row, gun up and ready to fire. Taylor moved into position. The radio signal to Taylor had been simultaneously received by a helicopter waiting nearby, and the pilot started his engines.

Kenny jerked his head around. "What's that sound?" he shouted.

Dean yelled back, "That's the relocation vehicle. As soon as I hit him, we will have five minutes to get him loaded and on oxygen; or he could smother—especially if I should hit him in the upper torso."

Kenny's face went white. "Dean, this is a joke. Man that's no . . . ."

Dean saw Terry running toward the woods straight for the gruesome eight-footer. He said, "No time to talk." He fired.

Terry looked back and saw Dean holding a gun. He ran past Taylor and hit the ground, covering his head. Taylor slowly lumbered forward toward Dean and Kenny, with big steps at first, followed by hesitant stagger steps. Finally he slumped slightly, stopped, and fell. The helicopter rose from its hold across the highway and moved toward Taylor. Kenny stood still as if transfixed by fear, his mouth wide open. Terry lay motionless, still covering his head against a second shot. Larry Wayne was hot-footing it down the last bean row toward his pickup a quarter mile away, jam box in tow, trailing a faint "Aarrrggkk, Aarrrggkk."

Dean radioed the helicopter, "There he is boys. Take him away." The copter landed near Taylor, and the crew carefully loaded him inside. The pilot saluted Dean and the copter lifted off.

Kenny was still functioning on adrenaline. "Do you think the monster will survive? The dart looked like it hit the big artery in his neck."

"As best I could tell, the dart only hit near the jugular vein. I figure the monster lost no more than a pint of blood." Actually, the dart was placed ahead of time, sealed into a pouch of crimson gel. A quick pinch had released the red liquid for effect. "That monster is tough. He will be back to normal by the time he reaches Australia."

Taylor's clothes, personal effects, and rental car would sit six blocks from Monica's Place in Shreveport in a residential area that allowed on-street parking. The street was always full, and the car wouldn't be noticed until dust from construction revealed that it had not been moved for weeks. By then, blood planted on the back seat headrest and door would be dry.

Eventually, an investigator would find the blood, cuts in the seat and armrest, and the box cutter. No other clues about Taylor Nicholas would ever be found. His disappearance would be explained as a kidnapping. Periodic review would never move the case forward.

Kenny and Terry were able to track down Larry Wayne. They headed to the diner to meet Dean for lunch. They were ahead of the crowd. The place was quiet except for the waitress sliding pieces of pie into a glass display near the register. The desserts circled a large uncut coconut carved with the likeness of a Boggy Creek Monster. A small knotty-pine shelf-unit on the wall offered Fouke Monster T-shirts and caps for sale. Twenty different types of caps and hats decorated the room. The picture on only one cap resembled Taylor's costume. The other caps and the T-shirts had images of Terry's gorilla.

The sun was almost overhead as Dean scooted into a booth with the three juniors. When the waitress arrived with her order pad, he said with a grin, "Lunch is on me. You boys eat up." He told the waitress, "I'll have the special and tea." He motioned to Terry.

"I'll have the same, but with a Coke." Kenny and Larry Wayne chose Pepsi, burgers, and fries.

Dean said, "Well, boys, I have to hand it to you. You really spoofed the old pro. I'll keep you in mind if I ever need creative team members."

Kenny replied, "We've been renting that costume on full-moons off and on for four years. That's about all the excitement we have around here. We first talked the school's custodian into wearing it. But he was so slow he almost got caught by a Rottweiler. Since then, Terry has been the gorilla. We didn't know there was actually a Fouke Monster. Really, we didn't. We had no idea we would lure the real monster into the open. How'd you know he was here?

"Well, since we're 'fessing up, I'll tell you. A few months ago a wildlife officer who lives down on the Sulfur River put a homing signal device into his right hindquarter. He's been tracked by satellite since."

Larry Wayne perked up. "Who was the officer? We might know him."

"Don't remember. I just saw his name in a report."

Terry said, "I know guys! The daughter of the author of *The Legend of Boggy Creek* . . . . She's married to a wildlife officer and can probably find out for us."

They had met their match. Dean was leaving them a trail to run. The pranksters had been checkmated; but the adventure only showed they were always in on the action.

The morning had kept Dean preoccupied. He needed to call Karla. Before leaving Fouke, he used a pay phone to check in with her.

She had been marking time waiting for his call. The phone rang while she was outside emptying trash. She raced indoors to answer, a little out of breath. "Hello."

"Hey lady, you'll never guess what I've been up to." Dean was upbeat.

"Where are you?"

"I'm about to leave Fouke, home of the Boggy Creek Monster. I just caught that critter and shipped him off to Australia. Check it out in tomorrow's paper."

The newspaper would treat the matter *tongue-in-cheek* like prior sightings and monster tracking events. In the same manner, Karla humored Dean. She visited a few minutes, then said goodbye. He could tell she thought he was drunk, holed up in a Bossier City motel after a day at the race-track. She didn't ask how much he had spent nor if he still had the red Humvee. He knew she would pray for him and thank God he was not in jail.

Chapter 11

Karla always read every article about Dean and saved the positive ones. That fall, she clipped and stored with her treasures the article from the society section of the *Arkansas Democrat/Gazette* about their marriage. Love had finally won over doubt; he was the one she wanted for life.

Their storybook wedding in Eureka Springs at Thorncrown Chapel and the lavish reception at the old Crescent Hotel were paid for by Dean's parents. Her teacher salary was not sufficient for entertaining their notable guests. She and Dean honeymooned at Niagara Falls, also courtesy of Dean's folks.

The new couple settled into life together in Grayville. Karla was no longer responsible for her siblings. Both were self-supporting and progressing with relationships of their own. She took a teaching position at Grayville Elementary School. The ensuing years were fulfilling and productive.

James Dean retired a few years after their marriage, and Dean was promoted to President and Chief Executive Officer. Dean owned twenty percent of the bank, his father twenty-nine. A group of investors owned a block of fifty-one percent under one proxy. Dean was their man. He was a laid back banker. He delegated routine functions to *the girls*. He handled public relations, investments, and *dealing*. Dean's version of bankers' hours fit him well. He would arrive about ten, get a report from his assistant, review the bad-check list, scan over-due loan files, and then look over the *Wall Street Journal* until time for lunch.

Most days, when he reached the town diner, he would be greeted outside by Jaws, a soup-bone hound. The dog was twelve years old and in bad health, but some said he was James Dean's favorite living thing outside his family. If Jaws lay against the screen door, no one dared wake him. The last time someone scooted him aside, he woke in a panic, jumped up on all fours, squared off in crisis mode, passed gas, and fell flat on his face—out cold. Since that time, townsfolk just used the rear door if he blocked the front. Nobody wanted to bring on the final fart and have to tell James Dean his dog was dead.

Every time Dean entered the diner, most heard him before they saw him. He was loud and moved like a bull in a china shop, making rounds of the customers. He spoke to each person about some detail of his or her life. Even out-of-towners caught a bit of his outgoing spirit and enthusiasm. He would say, "How ya'll doin'?" or, "What's goin' on?" then add, "Welcome to Grayville." He had a good heart. Invariably, he would pick up someone's tab— usually for a single mother or one of the little old ladies always there.

Once, a weathered farm wife in a sack-print dress told him her grandson had just been diagnosed with full-blown AIDS. The youth, a hemophiliac with a history of medical struggles, was threatening suicide. Dean sat down beside her, placed his huge right arm around her shoulder, buried his head in her straggly grey hair, and cried like a baby. That evening, he rode his four-wheeler four miles up West Boston Mountain just to give the boy a ride.

Dean was First Bank in the minds of Grayville's citizens. The bank contributed to the school, 4-H Club, Scouts, booster clubs, and other fund-raisers. "First Bank donated $1500," might be the report. Or someone might say, "You can count on Dean every time. We'll soon have that ten-thousand dollar scholarship." Oldsters counted on him, teenagers laughed and cut up with him, and men wrestled around and kidded with him. But all attested to his generosity.

Because of his position at the bank, he and Karla lived in a *glass house*. With her open and engaging personality, Karla quickly adjusted. The scrutiny was normal for Dean; he grew up that way. But after he married, though his weekend jaunts continued, he was more cautious and less cavalier about them. Karla worked at accepting his need for adventure. And Dean worked to keep her curiosity at bay.

Weekends when Dean was in town, he and Karla would usually attend church and spend Sunday afternoon together after a quiet meal at home. But one Sunday, when he planned to be away the next week, he suggested they eat out. "Karla, let's go over to A.Q. for lunch. That would give us a little more time together. Could you handle the new one in Fayetteville?"

"That would be great. No cooking. No dishes. We'll have time to talk." There was the usual Sunday line. But they knew the menu and were ready to order when a booth came available. Dean was soon occupied with an enormous yeast roll and butter. Karla nibbled on a roll and took in the view while they waited on their meal. From her seat, she could see the arboretum on the west end and the mural on the north wall.

The mural depicted the original 1930's A.Q. Chicken House in Springdale. Wagons were parked along the south end; horses at hitching posts faced north. The yard was scraped clean, except for clusters of nut grass. A tumblebug was headed across, back feet up on its take. Butterflies flitted about window boxes of multicolored

flowers at the entrance. The background was woods—
nothing past the restaurant. Narrow wagon wheels had
rutted the dirt road. Two puppies and their momma
trailed the rail-fence property line; they had worn a path
foraging bits of chicken.

Dean slathered butter on a second roll. Karla said, "If I
can go first, I have some questions."

"So it's finals, huh?" He tried to put a humorous
spin on wherever she was going with this. "What do I do
if I flunk, Teach?" Just then their food arrived. Dean
breathed in the aroma and smiled. He grabbed Karla's
hand and voiced a brief thanks for their meal and the
time together. Then he started on his fried chicken.
Crispy flakes of fried batter dusted Dean's plate as he
took a bite.

Karla toyed with her fork a moment. "Dean, I'd like
to know more about those weekends of yours that ended
tragically. Could we take them one at a time, and you
explain what happened and why?"

"Fine, Honey. Shoot." He hoped this wasn't driven
by jealousy. *Monogamous for life* was a commitment they
had made at a seminar their third year of marriage. He
was always troubled when Karla learned about women
accompanying him and his friends. He did what he could
to reassure her. He just couldn't tell her the truth.

But she wasn't on a witch hunt. "For starters,
you never told me about your pheasant hunt at Ness
City, Kansas, the week of Thanksgiving in 1982. I just
remember you said your buddy got juiced in the bathtub
and had to be airlifted for treatment. What really
happened, Dean?"

Ron Austin

"That guy was a risk taker. He was always trying to make the impossible happen. Well, he tried one too many on that trip."

"And . . . ."

"We had gone to eat on Friday after a long day's hunt. The night before, we had bathed first and got back so late that we decided to go like we were. Actually, we didn't look that bad. We hunted with coveralls or bib-overalls over our clothes to make us warmer and to keep the snow from getting us wet. We shed our outer layer, secured the birds and guns, jumped into the vehicles, and raced to the truck stop. My team won the race, so we had our pick of the tables.

On the way back this guy, Dave, decided to do a little daredevil stunt. He strapped his feet down with a bungee cord and rode standing on the front bumper. The temperature had dropped to thirty-nine when we left the truck-stop heading back. He rode like that all the way to the hotel, yelling and hollering the whole time.

By the time we got back, Dave was so cold we feared he might have hypothermia. We gave him the first draw of hot water, figuring he could warm up quicker and avoid problems. He was tougher than we thought. As soon as he got in his room, he grabbed his hair dryer to use as a heater while bathing; but there were no electrical outlets in our rooms. He found an extension cord in the custodial closet, then went downstairs and borrowed a screw-in receptacle. He removed the single bulb from the cord swinging in the center of the room and screwed in the receptacle. He plugged the extension cord into the receptacle. He dragged the extension cord into the bathroom, connected the hair dryer, pulled a loop in the cord, and hung the dryer from a nail above the sink at the end of the tub. Then he turned the dryer on."

Karla was leaning forward, listening intently. Dean stopped for a long drink of water. She asked, "So then what happened?"

"The lights blinked then went off after a loud *clunk* and the sound of glass breaking. I charged through our connecting door and found him out cold in the tub. The breaker had been blown, so all I had was street light. I saw the extension cord and unplugged it. I pulled him out, laid him on the bed, and gave him CPR. When his pulse was near normal, I ran downstairs and called for help.

First-responders came in an old Cadillac hearse. When we reached the hospital, he was airlifted to Wichita. Hospital staff said they thought the helicopter was out of Fort Riley at Junction City. I looked for his obituary. Never saw it. Never heard from him and haven't been able to contact him. It's a mystery, Karla."

"Sure seems that way to me, too." She had finished eating and looked around the room. Turning back to Dean, she said, "The crowd has let up, and there's no push for this booth. Tell me about the hunt. I've never been to west Kansas, but I've heard the little towns there are still just like cowboy times."

"Sure, we don't have to hurry. Let me see. We met at Van Buren on Wednesday evening, loaded my van and a station wagon and drove all night. We got there just after seven in the morning, and nothing was open. We ate peanut butter and jelly sandwiches, Vienna sausage, cheese slices, crackers, and pickles for breakfast. We hunted from eight-thirty to noon and ate the same thing for lunch—this time on the roadside between fields. I also ate my share of Tums and Rolaids."

Karla grinned. He always ate what he wanted, then thought about how he would be affected. That was Dean.

"We had permission to hunt on a farm of over forty-thousand acres owned by a large extended family. None of the bunch liked pheasant, considered them pests. The patriarch of the clan was near ninety and still in charge. He told us, 'Kill them all, we don't care. Just close the gates behind you, and watch out for my cattle.'

There was a fourteen-inch snow on Tuesday before Thanksgiving. Temperatures reached forty-five on Wednesday, but drifts and banks of snow more than five-feet-deep remained. We literally plowed through as we walked—the snow sometimes up to our waists; and we sweated like mules. The surface of the snow had melted and refrozen into a seal millimeters thick. Our boots kept a steady rhythm: *crack*, breaking the crisp ice; then *crunch*, forming our footprints. By the time the day was over, we had gotten six limits and three illegal hens. Not bad for seven novice pheasant hunters and one old pro! The pro got more than his share, but we'd never tell.

I was selected to handle the money. Each of us contributed one hundred dollars to the kitty for motel, meals, and gasoline. We paid for our own license fees and shells and were responsible for personal expenses. When we reached the hotel, the others told me, 'Go in there and get us a good deal on some rooms. We'll stay out here and pluck these birds and pack them in ice.'

Karla, you wouldn't believe that place. The lobby was small, but double swinging doors led to a bar just like the one at the Long Branch Saloon in Gunsmoke, a real mahogany bar. But, before you get ideas, I'll tell you. The bar was non-alcoholic. There was root beer on tap, soft drinks, and café mocha with whipped cream and sprinkles. Anyway, I went to the registry counter and said, 'We'd like some rooms. There are eight of us, and we plan to stay two nights. What's the charge?' I was ready to negotiate.

The desk clerk piped back, 'Ninety-six dollars.'

I was going to have to pass the hat again if I spent forty-eight dollars on each room. I said, 'That takes about all my money. Is that the best you can do?'

She was a fast thinker. 'What did you have in mind, Davey Crockett?'

I said, 'Nothing in particular, I just didn't figure on paying forty-eight dollars a room. Maybe we could double up in the rooms and cut the cost in half.' I knew each room had only one double bed, but I wanted the clerk to mention that. I was going to suggest she cut the rate by fifteen dollars a room.

The clerk looked puzzled. She said, 'Forty-eight dollars a room . . . ? No, the charge is forty-eight dollars a night, for all eight rooms. Two nights at forty-eight makes ninety-six dollars.'

I couldn't believe what I was hearing. The rooms only cost six dollars each per night. I said, 'We'll take them.' I paid her, adding tax and a hefty tip of a dollar per hunter per night. The total came to one hundred twenty. I couldn't wait to tell the others. She got the keys and showed me the rooms. I understood why her rate was so low.

When I got back outside, one of the guys gigged me, 'Well, that took you long enough. We thought you had gone on up and hit the sack.' But they perked up on hearing our deal. I told them, 'Boys, we each get our own private room. The beds are antique—canopy, feather mattress on coil springs and slats. The bathtub is retro too—the kind on legs, ornate and gold etched. I'm talking real old west. The rooms also have a couch, card table, and four chairs. Some of the furnishings may date back to the eighteen hundreds. Mind you, the only phone is downstairs. The only television is downstairs too—black and white, with rabbit ears. But, hey, guys we're here to hunt.'

Any other time, I would have impressed them with my bargaining. But we were dog tired. We just gathered our gear and filed in like trail hands after a hard cattle drive. We soon found out that hot water was limited. The tubs were deep and held a bather and more than fifteen gallons of water. After two tubs were filled, the slow pokes had to wait on hot water or bathe in cold. After we cleaned up, we were famished. I asked the desk clerk about restaurants.

'None open on Thanksgiving. You'll have to run up the road to find something open.'

'How far is "up the road?"'

'The truck stop will be open south of I-70 at WaKeeney. The food is good and the people friendly. Take 283 North; you'll be there in about forty-five minutes if you step on it. Nobody will bother you.'

Forty-five minutes up the road we crossed into the third county and saw a sign that read *I-70 15 Miles*. One of the guys asked, 'How long would it take if we just poked along? We've been running seventy.' He got no answer, just a nod of the head and an 'Uh huh.'

Actually, the trip was interesting. Pine tree wind-rows sectioned off farms like a checkerboard; black lines from far-away points converged at feedlots on corners bordering the roads. Large round Visqueen-covered hay bales surrounded well-fed registered cattle. Many were standing, asleep, huddled close to the hay. The lots held feed bins, water troughs with electric circulators to keep ice from forming, and salt blocks at each end. Across hills and down slopes, stalk teepees provided cover for hundreds of pheasant and grouse foraging for food. And through the mist, the setting sun stroked the sky red, blue, green and yellow. Karla, that sky was absolutely beautiful!"

She missed her cue to buy into the description. She was thinking about the bathtub tragedy. "Dean, why do so many of your friends end up hurt or killed? Are you accident prone, careless, or just unlucky? How many has it been now, twenty?"

He shrugged her off. "You worry too much. Everyone who is active and alert could tell tales about accidents and mishaps. I'm just more active and observant. Pick up the paper. Every time there's an accident there must be at least three and maybe up to a hundred people affected."

"Yes, but it seems there's always mystery involved with yours."

"That's just your imagination, Karla. What other questions do you have for me?"

She was ready. "Tell me about the Big Island incident, the submarine at the Bluffs, the drive-by shooting in Detroit, and the Lake St. Claire sailboat. Those should about get us to suppertime—if they don't run us out." She smiled, daring him to renege.

The waitress stopped by and asked, "Would you like coffee?"

Dean looked at Karla. She nodded. He replied, "Two, black. Thank you. And bring me a slice of apple pie with ice cream."

Karla said, "Add a scoop of ice cream for me."

The waitress left, and Dean launched into his next tale. "Big Island was simply a case of bad timing. We flew down for a weekend of deer hunting. The strip was muddy from recent rains, and the plane bogged down when the pilot tried to taxi close to his Jeep. We left the plane and hiked the last hundred yards. By the time we got there, I realized I'd left my billfold in the plane, so I headed back to look for it. The others went on to camp.

Just as I cleared the woods, about to head toward the plane, two men pulled a bass boat up to the sandy bank, rolled out a black plastic sack about six feet long, and sped off down the river. I hid until they rounded the bend, then I ran to investigate. Inside was a woman in her late thirties who was obviously seriously hurt. She was wearing hiking clothing and boots. Her breathing was shallow, and she was bleeding from her ears. I feared she might die. I ran to the plane, turned on the radio, and called for help. Medics came in a helicopter and picked her up. I never did hear who she was or what had happened."

Coffee and dessert arrived, but Dean didn't miss a beat. He was telling another adventure. He lifted his fork, pointed it for emphasis then started on his pie. The first taste prompted a brief "Mmmmm, that's good;" but he kept right on, finishing his stories between savored bites.

Karla was so focused that her last spoonful of ice cream melted. She pressed for one more answer. "Dean, tell me about Jamie Fox."

Dean looked at her for signs she knew more than she was letting on. He thought, "Where did she come up with that?" But he simply shook his head and said, "Karla, that one is a mystery even to me."

"But, Dean, from what I've heard you knew Jamie better than anyone."

Dean didn't like where this was going. "So who's talking about me and Jamie?" He focused on the crumbs left on his plate, slowly scooping them into a pile and onto his fork. He couldn't let on he knew anything.

Jamie had moved to Grayville just two years before. He purchased seventeen hundred acres for a homestead because he liked privacy. He planted a garden, ran a few cows, and hunted the wildlife—mostly deer, turkey and dove. He opened an account at the bank and stopped by Dean's office occasionally to chat. Only he and Dean knew this was interfacing for his Tuesday night Bridge assignment.

Jamie was a road-builder from Mobile, Alabama. He retired the year he moved to Arkansas, leaving the business to his oldest son. Government contracts for roads required pre-bid homework. Jamie had always traveled to Washington, D.C., for long weekends several times a year to lobby and to keep current of upcoming bid-letting. His first month after retirement was spent there to prepare for the transition from him to his son, and for that mother of all competitive events, the bidding of road and bridge contracts with the federal government.

On Monday, following Jamie's last weekend in D.C., his oldest son died in a freak accident on the job. The young man had been alone, digging a drainage ditch alongside Highway I-10 six miles east of the tunnel. He was found lying in the cab of the crane with the motor running and the bucket sunk deeply in the dirt. His pulse was barely attainable and estimated to be forty-six. His respiration was shallow and intermittent. Jamie was notified immediately. Soon a huge bright green helicopter arrived and lowered a platform. Green-clad paramedics promptly secured the injured man for a medical evacuation. Investigators found no electrical service cuts and no broken gas lines. No cause could be determined.

Jamie and his wife traveled to Mobile for their son's funeral. They kept to themselves afterward. Jamie had just finished digging post holes and putting up a new fence, when he told a teller at the bank he and his wife would be out of town a while. He said they just needed to get away. Most assumed they headed to be with family in Mobile. But, sometime later, a relative contacted the bank and reported they had disappeared on a sailboat trip to an island off the coast of North Carolina. Newspapers reported that their boat was found, but relatives could find no trace of the injured airlifted from the scene.

Karla had been watching Dean operate on the crumbs on his plate. She laughed. "Dean, you don't have to scrape up every crumb. If it's that good, order another piece. I'm waiting for you to look up. You asked me a question. And the answer is that I was in the bank after word got out about Jamie's disappearance. The tellers weren't busy, and we were just talking. His name came up. They said you were the only one in town with whom he ever spent any time.

Dean let go of the knot building in his stomach. "Well, honey, he was a major depositor. You know that I do my best to keep our customers happy. Jamie and I hit it off when he first came to the bank. He'd come by once in a while to tell me what he was doing to his place. If my time with him was major, he was a lonely man."

Karla smiled. "Well, I just had to ask. I wondered if you'd ever heard anything more about him."

He quickly changed the subject to the field trip she had scheduled for her class. She immediately put on her teacher glow and began telling him more than he wanted to know. He motioned for the waitress. She brought their ticket, and he paid out of cash he had drawn for the week ahead, adding a nice tip for their campout in the booth.

Chapter 12

Grayville was a typical small town. Decades before, outsiders exaggerated that the sidewalks rolled up at night. There was never anything going on. In many ways, the town was unchanged. But Friday and Saturday nights were different; downtown Grayville was exciting, loud, and often illegal. The square—the favorite hangout for teenage toughs and their broads—was always abuzz with cruising street rods, motorcycles, rollerblade quartets, and foot traffic. The shadows hid pot smoking, funneling beer, and sex with about anyone who would drop their drawers. Local law officers did what they could to thwart misbehavior and protect the young people from themselves.

Week nights were still *ho-hum*. Yet every Tuesday night a local informant watched the square. Armed with a micro-recorder in his shirt pocket, he made a verbal and a written account of activity overnight. At six in the morning, he would ease down to the local cafe as soon as it opened and get a booth. Dean's first order of business each Wednesday morning was to meet him there.

The report's format was always the same: *Blue Chevy Blazer, two-thirty, South on 34 to Bridge, Tag #BTX T94, Arkansas; Green Two-tone '94 Continental, two-fifty, South on 34 to Bridge, Tag #OTZ 111, Missouri; Black 4x4 Dodge Dakota Pickup . . . .* The informant wasn't told what the information meant to Dean or why these vehicles were in town that time of night and only on Tuesdays. He also wasn't told about the connection of these vehicle owners to felonious activity in thirteen mid-western and southern states. These contacts met only at the annual World Series games and the NBA playoffs, where their deals were made. Any adjustments came with their orders on Tuesdays. Codes, not names, were used by all involved parties.

Grayville rarely festered with more than petty theft. Residents were shocked when a man who lived just outside town was arrested for operating a stolen car ring and chop shop. His wife, who taught with Karla, was greeted by the sheriff one morning when she stepped outside for the morning paper. Within minutes, she and her husband were whisked away for questioning. That evening, Dean listened keenly to Karla's report of the talk around school. Apparently, other teachers knew the husband had been buying late model vehicles and breaking them down into parts.

His shop was in a dead-end valley; a rock mountain walled the valley off from the rest of his three hundred acres. The shop was accessible only through a natural gap in the rock. The three-acre shop area lay a good thirty feet lower than the nearest terrain. The shop was at the center of a circular driveway around the perimeter. Few locals had actually been there; some had seen it from the hillside while hunting. When word got out, others went to look just because they were nosey.

Some three years after he sold the first parts, a neighbor asked about his business. He said, "Most of the cars I get are flood-damaged. They can't be sold whole; they've been totaled by insurance companies and can't legally be reinsured. There's little profit after overhead; but it pays the bills." He said he would bid on a lot of ten or fifteen; if he got the bid, he would contract their delivery to his shop that evening. By the next morning his trailers—loaded with engines, transmissions, tires, axles, frames, hoods, and other useful parts—would head to Tulsa to be sold at auction. The neighbor said, "I bet the work is fast and furious. I would like to come out one night and watch your operation." The owner had not responded.

After the arrest, his scheme was the focus of conversation around town. The man's wife was not involved and gave an honest report of all she knew of her husband's business dealings. She was released uncharged but still was *damaged goods* in the minds of most around Grayville. The day she returned to school, a telephone call disrupted dinner at the home of the president of the Grayville school board. The caller demanded, "What're you boys gonna' do about that teacher involved in them stolen vehicles? We don't want that kind teaching our kids. It don't matter if she did get her schoolin' here."

This caller was only one of those who regularly complained. Each week three or four board members received calls about something—never anything positive. But this time, the calls continued through late evening, reaching every board member; and the subject was the teacher. Some called on their own initiative, and others were frenzied into action by the first caller. The board president ate dinner cold at nine-fifteen. He sucked Tums from the first call at six-thirty to nine that night. He had no heartburn, but his ears burned for almost three hours.

The buzz about the chop shop didn't settle down for weeks. The board had no reason to take action against the teacher, and she returned to school after a couple days personal leave. Karla told Dean she wasn't sure she could handle the pressure if she were in that position. He assured her, "Don't worry your sweet little head. You've got nothing to worry about." But unanswered questions plagued her.

Chapter 13

Dean's Bridge assignments usually followed a schedule
set weeks in advance. But one situation out of his region
arose unexpectedly. He was drawn in because of his
connections. He had attended a banking conference
in Denver three years before, where he met Rodney
Simmons, who handled public relations for the State of
Colorado. For four years, Rodney had been an aide to the
senior senator from Colorado. Dean and Rodney golfed
together during the conference weekend; and the next
year Rodney invited Dean back for the boat races in the
rapids near Salida. Most recently, the two had been
in Washington, D.C., at the same time and had lunched
together.

Rodney had worked alongside the senator in
acquiring financial support from a bi-partisan group of
Denver and Colorado Springs businessmen involved in
pharmaceuticals. He handled a controversy that arose
over the premature release of test results for an
experimental cancer drug. Later, he facilitated approval
of that medicine by the Food and Drug Administration.
This new drug promised millions in profit for Colorado
investors.

But after FDA approval, the senator received a tip
from a Japanese import/export executive about Toshi
Ichimura, the research lead in the drug's development.
Reportedly, when Ichimura was exposed for unethical
practices in Japan he had transferred his work to
the United States. The businessman, Mr. Otake, had
testified about Ichimura importing components banned
from medical applications. The senator assigned
Rodney to an undercover operation, and he was making
inroads with Ichimura's staff when the man died. In an
apparently unrelated incident, Ichimura was electrocuted

at an upscale hotel as he tried to enter his room after a morning jog.

His death appeared to be accidental, but the inquest afterward was inconclusive. A conduit for two-hundred-twenty volt electricity ran through the wall on which Ichimura's room door hung. In recent repairs, the conduit and wiring had been damaged, sending electricity to the metal door. The facts suggested that when Ichimura inserted his key, body sweat from his jog provided conduction to complete the circuit and kill him.

One of Ichimura's lab assistants reportedly knew enough to head up the work. However, since the drug was not under production, financial supporters dropped the project, closed the lab, and put the property up for sale. The next day, the senator received a phone threat in a muffled Asian accent: "Message for Rodney Simmons. Me Ichimura friend. You responsible for death. We avenge him." The senator contacted the Chief of Staff in the President's office. Rodney was at risk. Mr. Otake was also likely in danger.

Dean canceled a speech before the school booster club to be in Colorado early that Friday afternoon. He checked into a hotel, unpacked, and called a limo service. A Japanese chauffeur, Meito, soon tapped on his door. Dean asked him in, looked both ways to make sure the hall was clear, and shut the door. He called room service and ordered dinner. He and Meito ate while they outlined plans for Sunday.

Afterward, still early in the evening, Meito left and brought his limousine to the front of the hotel. The concierge announced the limo's arrival, and Dean came right down. With quiet dignity, Meito opened the passenger door, and Dean took a seat in the rear.

Meito drove a circuitous route through the city and parked outside an exclusive club. Dean tried to keep a low profile, leaned back, hat over his eyes like he was sleeping.

In moments, a Sumo wrestler leaving the club stopped and addressed Dean's driver in Japanese. He said, "Komban wa. Ika'ga desu ka?" [Good evening. How are you?]

"Ha, ari'gato gozaimasu. Anata wa?" [Fine, thank you. And you?]

The big guy was always doing well. "Aikawarazu." [Same as always.]

From this point, what they said was not only in Japanese, but in code, should anyone be in earshot. The wrestler said, "Osore irimasu. Sumimasen. Onegai shimasu. Sakuban no shimbun wa mo yomimashita ka?" [I'm sorry to trouble you. I make a request of you. Have you read last night's paper yet?]

"Hai. Sakuban watakushi ga shimbun o yonde ita tokoro e Otake-san ga asobi ni kita no desu." [Last night when I had just been reading the paper, Mr. Otake came to call.] "Asatte Amerika o tatsu hazu da kara, sakuban watakushi no tokoro e asobi ni kita no desu." [He's supposed to leave the day after tomorrow, so he came to visit me last night.]

In their brief discussion, the wrestler reminded Meito, "Otake-san no shihai suru kaisha wa kaigai e iroiro na shinamono o yushutsu shite imasu." [Mr. Otake's company exports all sorts of goods overseas.] He reiterated the importance of this assignment and asked Meito if he had everything set up.

"Hai. Watakushi wa asatte, issho ni hikojo e itte Otake-san no hikoki ga tatsu made ni matsu tsumori na n desu." [Meito assured him he would be at the airport the day after tomorrow and wait until Mr. Otake's plane took off.]

Meito drove a different winding route back to Dean's hotel, watching to be sure he was not followed. On the way, he and Dean discussed his conversation with the Sumo wrestler and made minor adjustments to their plans. On arrival, he formally opened Dean's door and stood respectfully in place until he entered the hotel.

As promised, Meito was watching as the private plane taxied down the runway. In seconds, a blast at the end of the taxiway was heard in the terminal nearly five kilometers away. The only passenger, Mr. Otake, had been sitting on the right side near the blast area. A gaping hole was visible as fire trucks and rescue personnel surrounded the plane. A helicopter descended into the melee and lowered its side ramp. Meito pulled binoculars from his pocket and placed them up to his eyes. He focused but could barely make out the victim.

A policeman and reporter nearby were discussing the incident. Meito walked over to them and asked what had happened. He played the normal bystander—a chauffeur there to pick up a passenger. The policeman told him he was not allowed to give out any details and asked him to move along. Meito sauntered off and called Dean with his report. Dean checked out of his hotel and flew back to Arkansas.

Dean was scheduled to attend the Renaissance Renewal on Hilton Head Island in South Carolina all the next week. Karla was going along for fun. School started in two weeks. She rarely traveled with him during the school year, so this would be a mini-vacation for her. He enjoyed having her with him. She was always just herself, refreshing to those who tired of name droppers and fame seekers. Her genuine interest in others drew out even the stand-offish.

After dinner their first night, they were conversing with others at their table when Dean noticed Rodney Simmons nearby. He had expected Rodney would attend. He excused himself and went over to speak with him. He was gone just a short time and rejoined Karla and the others at their table. He was soon into a description of ice-fishing in Alaska. When the banquet room began to empty, they said, "Good night," and walked toward the elevator. Dean listened absentmindedly as Karla bubbled about the evening. His mind was already occupied.

The week passed quickly with the conference consuming most of each day for Dean. Karla was involved in the luncheons and special outings for spouses, so she kept busy. But the last day, she opted out of the planned agenda. To this point, she and Dean had spent his free time together. But, on their last afternoon in town, he wanted time outdoors, and she wanted to experience shopping on Hilton Head Island.

Dean was attending sessions all morning. When she awoke she lingered in the shower. Afterward, she dressed and called room service for breakfast. She ate heartily. After lazing over her coffee a few minutes, she requested transportation to the nearest mall.

There would be a few minutes wait, so she opened her diary and began writing. This was her therapy. She had made entries almost every day since second grade—even if just a word or a phrase. She wasn't sure how many books she had filled. She kept them in her closet behind boxes of shoes. Almost no one knew about them.

Curiously, once while waiting outside the county courtroom, a reporter had said, "You know, if one kept a diary, days like today might lead to a special entry. Don't you agree? I mean since Dean is on the witness stand instead of at the defense table." He was there to testify for one of the bank's customers about cattle values. Karla had mumbled sounds that indicated agreement and disinterest. Deciding this idle talk was planned, she had excused herself, rounded the corner, and slipped outside. She had sipped coffee in a diner across the street until the reporter wandered outside, looked around, and left in a cab. Remembering now, she shuddered at the idea of her innermost feelings being exposed. The phone rang. The Concierge told her that the limousine was ready.

She mostly window-shopped, more interested in observing the latest styles and the eclectic shops than purchasing anything. At a small bookstore she bought Steele's latest book, *The Accident*. She stopped for a lunch of quiche and raspberry tea, and then backtracked to a little shop for a jacket she had decided on. She returned early to the hotel to relax before the banquet that evening.

Dean grabbed a quick lunch when his last session ended and headed out. After ten years, he was a pro at maximizing his free-time with beach activity and water sports. He had tried everything—parasailing, riding the ocean on a giant tricycle, surfing, swimming, boating, wave-running on jet skis, bungee-jumping and snorkeling. His first trip, he had bungee-jumped just to impress girls in the crowd. But he enjoyed the thrill of the jump and eventually developed a style. His artistic form often won when he competed with the guys.

His choice for the last afternoon was to meet Rodney Simmons for parasailing. Breathtaking view, sunshine, and sparkling water enhanced the thrill of gliding on the wind, free like a bird. Completing their run, they circled the area four times and made one approach to the beach to size up the landing site and check out the wind. The boat operators taught hand signals to all riders. Dean's signal for the final approach was picked up by the boat crew and spotters on the beach. They were banking from the north into a westerly wind at fifteen miles per hour, perfect for landing.

Suddenly, Dean was alone in the parasail. Rodney's harness lay limp in the double seat. He was falling thirty feet to the blue-green ocean below. He looked like a skilled acrobat, sliding free in an upside-down swan-dive style, hands out, feet together. He was perpendicular to the water, perfectly straight with his hands to his sides and his head up and tilted slightly back when he hit the water and submerged.

The water was forty-feet deep at the shallowest point there, over a hundred yards from shore; he was headed for deep dark water. His life jacket met only minimum safety standards, with a tight fit and no resistance to the water, almost like a wet suit. Three minutes is a long time to stay under; Dean carefully timed him. He knew Rodney's limits.

The boat operator wisely kept Dean airborne; his hand signals directed lifeguards to the area. After twenty minutes, Rodney was found floating on his back. He was taken directly to a first aid hut on the south side county pier. Yellow caution flags rippled above. The rescue helicopter did not land on the pier but hovered overhead, a good two hundred yards above the beach. The swirl from a beach landing could have sandblasted bystanders. The helicopter dropped a platform on two cables; the cable ends were inverted *Y's* attached at the platform corners. Within five minutes, Rodney was secured in place and raised into the helicopter's open door.

Meanwhile, Dean had landed and was observing the scene. He overheard a policeman nearby comment, "Wow! That was quick. I've never seen such an efficient rescue in all my days on the force." His companion asked, "Did you notice the unique insignia on the bottom of that big bird?"

Dean heard his name called. "Dean! Hey there, Dean! Dean! Over here!" He slowly turned, and saw a young couple running toward him, the guy holding a video camera and the girl a writing pad. They appeared to be opportunist reporters. Their familiarity made him uneasy. When they reached him, a barrage of questions ensued.

"Who was your sailing partner? Was he hurt? Where was he from? Could you give us a statement about the accident and how badly hurt you think he may be?"

Dean knew how to duck questions. He carefully and tactfully explained that his friend came loose from his harness and accidentally fell into the ocean.

The reporters were persistent. "Where did they take him? And, what kind of rescue copter was that? Do you know?"

Dean did not tell them who the friend was nor how badly hurt he might have been. Nor did he discuss the helicopter. If anyone ever put all the clues together, his Bridge work would cease. He wondered if they were closing in. He excused himself, and headed for the pay phone at the refreshment center.

The phone rang at the hotel. Karla muted the television, reached for the receiver, and said, "Hello, this is Karla."

"Hey, Karla, I'm over on the County Pier. Rodney and I were parasailing; and somehow he fell out. A rescue team found him; he's headed to a trauma center on the coast. I'm coming in to clean up, but let's skip the closing banquet. I don't want to deal with people asking about this all night. Let's do dinner by ourselves."

"That's good for me, Dean. I'll be ready when you get here."

He sounded somewhat hyper. She did what she could to calm him, responding appropriately to such unexpected news. She had never met Rodney, had only seen him once across the room. Dean had pointed him out the first night of the conference as his next *victim*. Dean was forever pulling pranks. She had dismissed his comment as meaning he planned having fun at Rodney's expense.

That night, away from the conference, Dean was his usual confident self. They enjoyed a quiet meal and talked about fun times from the week. As Dean was scooping up his last bite of chocolate mousse, he began talking about his week ahead in Little Rock. At one point, he reached for Karla's hand and held it a moment. "Thanks for making reservations for me. One of these days, Karla, I need to take you to the Capitol Hotel for dinner. Their steaks are superb, and you know I know what I'm saying. But I'd like you to experience the service—waiters in tuxes, Karla. You deserve that." Then he winked at her. "But until then, I'll be there next week enjoying it for you."

Karla pulled her hand loose and lightly smacked his. She smiled. "I'll get my turn in Washington, D.C. You better plan something special."

The next day, Kerri Watson was reviewing the latest from the Associated Press—an article from *The Island Packet* headed, "President Arrives for Renaissance Renewal Finale." A sub-headline read: "Accident Mars Week." She focused on the description of an accident involving Dean off the coast of Hilton Head, South Carolina. Her heart began to beat faster.

Just days before, she had learned Dean was there. An article had come in about him and the week-long event: "Arkansas Native Attends Tenth Consecutive Renaissance Renewal." That article described the vacation conference for well-heeled politicians, professionals, entrepreneurs, and people of the arts. A few notables were quoted, and at the end was a brief paragraph about Dean Story and his years of involvement.

Kerri's skin tingled with excitement. She thought, "Maybe, just maybe, if I talked with the reporter who wrote the story run by the AP, I could get more details." She and Carl Lee packed their bags and took a red eye flight to South Carolina.

A rack of *The Island Packet* greeted them at the motel entrance. Kerri slid a copy into her briefcase. After settling in, she called the newsroom. She reached the reporter who had written about the parasailing accident. After they exchanged a few pleasantries, Kerri and Carl Lee were invited to lunch. Kerri thought, "Yes!" and graciously accepted. She charmed everything she could from the reporter, but when lunch was over she had gleaned only a couple details of interest. He had referred to the rescue helicopter as a *big green machine;* and he had said, "We never did find out where they took his body."

With the reporter's permission, Kerri had recorded their conversation. On the flight home, Carl Lee was sleeping, so she began to play through the tape. There they were again—the details that caught her attention. She turned off the recorder and leaned back, closing her eyes. She thought about other tragedies involving Dean. Suddenly, she sat straight up. The mystery was unraveling.

By the end of the next week, Kerri completed the second article. Part Two was a large spread in the Sunday newspaper. The chronology of tragic events connected to Dean was damning evidence. Statements attributed to families of the accident victims sketched a heart-breaking circle of life impact. There was no small stir among those who knew Dean and Karla. But calls to their residence went unanswered.

Chapter 14

On Monday morning, Grayville's schools were in session. The high school gym rang with the national anthem. Young voices pledged allegiance to the flag of the United States of America. The student assembly was underway. The principal took a step toward the microphone.

He was blindsided by the Student Council President, who stepped ahead of him and began to pray—for her principal and teachers and the student body as a whole in the new school year. She offered thanks for the school and for freedom of speech. Her "Amen" was echoed by students throughout the gym. The principal froze, not knowing whether to thank her, reprimand her, or just ignore her.

Before he could decide, the school secretary rushed onstage to him, whispering, "You have an urgent phone call. You can take it in the coach's office, Line one." A senior sponsor stepped in while he took the call. The superintendent had news. "Have you seen the morning paper? Dean and Karla Story have been killed in a plane crash. I just got my paper; a runner is bringing it over to you. You're going to have a tough job with the student body. Good luck."

The principal was thankful for the teachers who had given him some history on Dean and Karla. Because of them, he had a chance to plan a wise path forward. He knew Karla had taught most of these students. She and Dean were high profile at school activities. They were well known and loved in Grayville. He realized this was a crisis. He thought, "Do I step up to the microphone and read the headline? Do I paraphrase it? Should I prepare them, slowly explain, and then play it by ear?

When he had the newspaper in hand, he hurried to the microphone. He called the Student Council President back up to lead in a few moments of silence. He asked the teachers and staff to join him in an adjacent classroom for an impromptu meeting. When they heard the news, tissues were shared all around. He said, "I know this is a personal loss to many of you, and you may need to check out and go home. But if you can, please stay to help the students deal with this news."

The students were still silent when the principal rejoined them in the gym. The atmosphere was serious, and they sensed it. At the microphone, he bowed his head briefly to collect his thoughts. He looked up and lifted the newspaper in his right hand. "I have sad news. When I tell you what has happened, I want you to help each other. Please try to be composed, and feel free to express yourself to your friends. If you feel panic, go to a teacher or counselor. They are here to help. We will not have classes today. We're going to talk awhile."

He cleared his throat and read the headline, "Airplane Crashes and Disappears in Bermuda Triangle, Grayville Couple Feared Drowned." He added, "The Grayville couple were your friends—Dean and Karla Story." He slowly read the first lines of the article:

> Miami. A small twin-engine plane has disappeared in the Bermuda Triangle. Dean and Karla Story from Grayville, Arkansas, left Washington, D.C., about two o'clock yesterday afternoon en route to Bermuda. Local authorities hold no hope of finding survivors.

He stopped there. Commotion had already begun among the students. Sobbing and wailing could be heard. Members of the area crisis intervention team began to arrive. Team members were counselors, grief specialists and psychiatrists; all were specially trained for group crisis response. Word had spread in the community, and local church ministers and other community leaders showed up to work alongside the crisis team. Each quickly positioned to handle the stunned students.

The students' conversations were emotional and filled with questions: "Why haven't they found the bodies? Could they be alive? They haven't found the plane, have they? When will the funeral be? How will they have a funeral without the bodies?"

In some cases, students would just stare at the wall, or cry effusively and out of control, or vent with cursing to relieve pressure. Most difficult were the groups of six to eight eighth-grade girls who got high from the tragedy. Adolescent insecurity and fear combined with the inability to compose themselves to talk through the issue. They would cry at every statement from the group then run over one or two at a time to gather others to huddle and cry with them.

As the myriad of counselors met with students, new stories emerged about Dean Story, adding fresh color to the big man with the big heart. One student, in tears, said, "He gave me fifteen dollars to go on my first overnight basketball trip when I was a freshman. Otherwise I couldn't have gone; I didn't have any money for meals."

Karla also had the students' respect, and many told about her impact on them. A teary-eyed girl said, "Mrs. Story was my teacher. She made me learn my multiplication tables. She wouldn't take 'No' for an answer. I don't know how many recesses I spent on the wall because I wouldn't work on them. I'm so glad she didn't let me slide by."

Small town familiarity and trust are powerful credentials. Even the custodian was sought out by student helpers who worked under him. The fifth-period helper, who mopped the cafeteria and took out the slop, later said, "He was the first person I saw when I looked up, so I just went over and busted out crying. He helped me a lot."

That evening, the parents' overall opinion was, "This was the right way to handle our kids." Seventy-one of them called the board president to commend the school. A sense of community surged from the loss, and respect for the school multiplied.

Town loyalty eclipsed suspicions raised by Kerri Watson's articles. Grayville residents rose to the occasion to embrace their own. The memorial service for Dean and Karla shut down the town all afternoon. The church swelled with neighbors, co-workers, and friends. Chairs filled the aisles, and the crowd overflowed to the outside. For almost two hours, mourners streamed to the microphone to give personal eulogies. After the pastor's closing words, townsfolk lingered another hour reliving Dean and Karla moments. Everyone realized they were the essence of Grayville's story.

Kerri left Part Three of her series with the editor's secretary. She walked back to her cubicle and picked up the Associated Press article about the crash off Florida's coast. She re-read every word, focusing on the parts skipped at Grayville School:

> The plane had only recently been released for use. The state-of-the-art Cessna XLT170 was specially built and equipped for computer-controlled take-offs and landings. A recent *Washington Post* article reported liability

coverage of five million dollars per passenger for any accidents arising from plane failure. Though Dean Story was on hand to watch the plane's demonstration, sources have not disclosed how he gained permission to fly it to Bermuda.

A spokesperson for the company which designed the plane has said, "We aren't sure our plane disappeared. Without a plane to show, who's to know what kind of plane crashed; if in fact one did? There will be no further comment until confirmation that our plane was involved." He refused to give information about the plane's location, trips the plane had made, or the reported insurance package.

This convinced Kerri that she had nailed the situation with her upcoming expose'. Her third and last article was master reporting. She had artfully framed her theory that Dean Story was a drug kingpin. Circumstantial evidence was strong and convincing; prosecutors would be compelled to take a look. Arrest records from thirty reported deaths painted a demeaning caricature of Dean as an underworld money maker. She regretted he had not lived to face justice.

The series on Dean Story had been a challenge. She had beaten a path to the editor for regular reports; he had believed in her work and even wrote her series introduction. She had traveled the State extensively and had worn out two micro-recorders. Like a lawyer preparing for trial, she had taxed her creative ability, analytical skill, and investigative technique. Her credibility had earned an extensive list of unnamed sources in and around the State of Arkansas—which would be highly useful throughout her career. Her work was backed by a three-inch-thick portfolio of documents and a file box of photos, videos, and audio tapes—all directly involving Dean Story. She deserved a pat on the back.

The editor called Kerri to his office as soon as he was free. She walked in confidently, pumped for praise. He began with genuine admiration for her accomplishment, and gave kudos for her work ethic and energy. Then as she watched, a fret shoved down the corners of his smile. She heard *regret.* Outside pressure had squelched the series. Part Three would never see print. This was *not* what she had envisioned for her convincing report. She was caught cold. She managed to say, "Thank you sir. I know you are doing the right thing." Later, she had difficulty remembering anything he said. Reluctantly, and with a sense of loss, she filed away Part Three and her investigative report.

Chapter 15

From the moment their plane touched down, Karla was totally at ease. Not once in Dean's many weekends in D.C. had there been a tragedy, nor had Dean been implicated in wrong-doing. Their hotel's courtesy van picked them up at the airport and headed into heavy traffic.

Dean was in the mode of "Are we there yet?" but Karla was mesmerized. This was her first look at Washington, D.C. Like a child, she turned from side to side to take in the changing panorama outside the windows. She was almost disappointed when they reached the hotel. Their van entered the drive and approached the carpeted entrance, and doors closed on both ends of the drive-through. The enclosed space could accommodate an entourage of six to ten vehicles delivering passengers. The private entrance afforded safety and anonymity to arriving dignitaries.

Karla was taken aback when she and Dean were met at the door by a man who identified himself as the President's Chief of Staff. He escorted them through a lobby decorated in Renaissance era art. Southeast of the lobby, they entered a narrow hallway. There they were transferred to new guides, two young men dressed in crisp red, white, and blue uniforms. Karla noticed that the left breast pocket of their jackets displayed a unique green patch. Small talk and good-byes were the only conversation between the entrance and the narrow hallway.

Thirty feet ahead was an escalator; they rode down four levels to a mezzanine. They faced three doors—R-Team I, II and III. Dean had attended multiple meetings in the room marked, "R-Team I". Their guides opened the door to R-Team II, and Dean saw the auditorium inside for the first time. He and Karla were ushered to seats reserved for them in the midst of several dignitaries.

Dean's usual 130/80 blood pressure and pulse of 64 rose out of kilter. His pressure was more like 170/110 and his pulse over 100. His breathing was fast and shallow; his mind was racing. This was a big step. Would Karla be persuaded? Would she panic before the entire program was explained? What would happen when Dad was introduced? What would be the plan if she refused? He had signed an irrevocable contract with the BDI Director and Directors of both the FBI and the CIA.

A man stepped to the podium. "Ladies and gentlemen, we are meeting today for a report on one of the most successful governmental endeavors of all time and to recognize a key player in that success."

Karla knew they had gotten into the wrong line somewhere or she was dreaming. She pinched her arm. "Nope, I'm awake." She pinched Dean's arm. He pulled his arm away and said, "Ouch," giving her a quizzical look. He had not been loud enough to be disruptive, but he had captured the eyes of those on the small stage. "What are you doing?" he whispered.

She whispered back, "What am *I* doing? What are *we* doing?" She wondered if she had entered the *Twilight Zone*.

Dean softly said, "Shhhh." He admonished her under his breath, "Pay close attention," and returned his focus to the stage.

Karla had no idea why she was here. She was uninvolved, but she tried to listen to the speaker. As she did so, she began to hear words Dean had used: Recruitment, Bridge, Facilitator, Activator, and Renaissance. He had thrown the terms around with various connotations and hidden meanings. The speaker was clearly defining them; and she could tie most of them to events in Dean's life and roles he had filled. The speaker began an introduction.

"In 1950, the Naval Academy at Annapolis received a mere boy with test scores the highest ever recorded on criteria identifying prospects for the CIA and FBI. Applicant test results were routinely screened not only by them but by a newly formed organization, the Bureau of Domestic Intelligence, or BDI. The BDI requested a referral of this young man and subjected him to a battery of additional tests; his results were phenomenal. He transferred to BDI and entered two years of tough and intense training. He excelled in all aspects of their agent development program. He left a man."

From behind the stage curtain came a soft rustle, like house shoes on carpet. The speaker hesitated for a second then continued, "Before I introduce him, let me tell you that he has served his country well for more than thirty-seven years, all but two in his hometown of Grayville, Arkansas." Karla was involved now. He was talking about her State, her town! She caught her breath as the speaker continued.

"This man played a major role in one of the most eventful scenarios of crime-busting America will ever witness. In the last seventeen years, he handled thirty cases involving accidental death. He interfaced effectively with some of the most dedicated legal minds in the U.S. He has passed money to prosecutors and defense attorneys all over the country. Despite evidence of questionable involvement, he convinced lawyers on both sides that his client was innocent. Please rise, as we pay tribute to a great patriot, James Dean Story."

James Dean emerged from behind the curtain. The room resounded with applause. Now Karla was hyperventilating and holding tight to Dean's huge right biceps. The speaker continued. "In recognition of your service Agent Story, we hereby award you the greatest honor bestowed upon a member of the United States Bureau of Domestic Intelligence, the Presidential Merit Award for Domestic Peace."

James Dean approached the podium. He smiled at Dean and Karla. She thought, "He's not surprised to see me here. What's going on?"

Her father-in-law began to speak. "Thank you. I greatly appreciate this honor. I am pleased to have served our government in the fight against domestic crime. But after such a grand introduction, I must give you the truth about my start with BDI.

I graduated from high school in an old gym constructed in 1924 by the WPA. That night the place was packed, and my class was small. We were all thinking, 'Why such a crowd?' until the school board president announced the special guest for the evening. U.S. Senator William Fulbright was in Grayville, and he came because of me, to announce my appointment to the U.S. Naval Academy. He graded on the curve, or he might have skipped right over this old country boy.

The day I arrived at Annapolis, I was barely legal, having turned eighteen the week of graduation in June, 1950. The testing and training kept me busy those first two years in Washington, D.C. My work was demanding, and I had only three days off each month. I was single and a long way from home. On my days off, sometimes I would hop a cab to a suburban shopping center for lunch and a movie. Afterward, I would shop and people watch until time to eat again and go home.

I've never been good looking; but I managed to catch the eye of a waitress at the soda fountain where I ate burgers. We chatted, and I asked her out. We had to schedule our date a month ahead. During the wait, I was sure she would forget. But she didn't, and we began dating every month.

I'm not proud of it; but one thing led to another and soon she was pregnant. I was in the last couple weeks of my final year in D.C. when the baby was born. The mother wasn't an American citizen. Her parents were civil servants from one of the Scandinavian countries. They were scheduled to rotate back home the same year I completed the BDI program. We really didn't get to say goodbye. We promised to write.

I returned to Grayville and went right to work with my Dad at the bank. A young lady from a neighboring community came in one day. I had met her a few weeks before at the Albert E. Brumlee Gospel Sing at Parsons Stadium in Springdale. We spent time talking and learned we had many common interests. That day led to a short courtship, and we married within six months.

On the trip home from our honeymoon in Eureka Springs, she told me that she wasn't able to have children. That broke this old boy's heart. I was set on having a big family. I couldn't say a word.

The silence was unbearable, and so was the heat. When we came up on a watermelon field, I challenged her, 'I'll race you to the patch, and let's see who can steal the first one.' Watermelon is best on a hot day, especially if you just bust it and dig out the heart. That day when I bent over for the second big chunk, I got juice running into my sinuses. I started laughing. She started laughing. Then we were talking again. You see, we really loved each other.

I thought a lot about not having kids. Two sleepless nights later, I told her about the baby in Washington, D.C. She insisted we call to talk with the mother. We learned she had been given an ultimatum by her parents to leave the baby in America. We negotiated a settlement. We paid for her hospital expenses and for the baby's care up to that time and she let us adopt him. Who would have thought I would get to raise my own flesh and blood as an adopted son?

James Dean's lips were quivering. He paused until his emotions subsided. "I applaud my wife. I'm sorry she couldn't attend. That was impossible, because she doesn't know a thing about my career in BDI. And I can't tell her. She will never know."

Karla was putting pieces together more quickly than a puzzle on a snowy day. The last ones flew into place. There were details yet to be heard; but, plainly, Dean was in this up to his wallet-worn back pockets.

But the surprises weren't over. James Dean was still talking. "From 1952-75, I served as an occasional Bridge for sixteen cases. But my most satisfying experience came in the seventeen cases I worked as a Facilitator. As an agent of the BDI, I have had the privilege of serving my country and family concurrently. I would like to present my co-worker and son, Dean Story! Come up here, Dean. We are also honoring you today. You put your life and reputation on the line thirty times. And Karla, please come with him."

As they joined him on stage, James Dean began describing the contract Dean had signed, trading his and Karla's identities for new ones. Dean could scarcely breathe.

Karla had been gripping Dean's arm; now her knuckles turned white. The smile pasted on her face began to hurt. Her senses, her will, and her emotions were in violent upheaval. She had bought into Dean's unique lifestyle, or she would never have married him. She had meant her vow, "As long as we both shall live." But she couldn't have known she would one day have to give up everyone else in her life for him. At the same time, she was also exhilarated. Her respect for Dean and his father and her love and devotion to Dean were all exponentially magnified. Her head was throbbing. She had difficulty breathing.

James Dean had been talking all the while she fought within. Suddenly, she realized he was silent. All eyes were on her. She felt Dean reach to take her hand. His love lay fragile in her palm. A heart wrenching eternity passed. Finally, she knew. She gently cupped her other hand over his and looked up at him with tears in her eyes. She loved him. She could not refuse. Her genuine smile brought applause from everyone watching. Haltingly, James Dean concluded the private ceremony.

Photos were taken and developed; Dean, Karla and James Dean were given time to look at them. The pictures were then placed in an envelope along with an account of the entire event on video cassette, CD Rom, floppy diskette, and in print. The packet would be sealed and stored for forty-nine years before becoming part of the public domain.

After the program, the three of them had time together privately. Dean spoke first, "Dad, what can I say. I am so proud of you. What an honor. You know I love you. I love you, and I'm grateful for the life you've made possible for me. Please hold Mom real tight when you tell her I love her."

James Dean wisely replied, "Dean, I love you, too; but I'm not going to tell your mother that for you. You call her right now and tell her yourself before all the excitement begins. There's a phone in the corner. Use it."

Dean placed the call. Karla stood close by. She wanted to talk with his mother too. After just two rings, he heard his mother's familiar voice on the other end. He responded, "Hello, Mom."

"Dean, I'm so glad you called. I can relax now that I know you arrived safely. I'm so glad you and Karla have this time away together. When are you coming home?"

There was much to say. Dean struggled for composure. "We'll be back soon, Mom. Hey, I just called to tell you I love you. I was thinking today how much I appreciate all you have done for me. I want you to know that you're the best Mom a guy could ask for. I would do anything . . . ." Dean's voice trailed off as he was overwhelmed with memories of her love and care for him.

Dean was never one to hesitate, and he was rarely sentimental. She probed, "Dean, have you been drinking again?"

Tears were already streaming down his cheeks. He inhaled deeply, reaching for inner strength. "No, Mom. I've just realized that I need to tell you more often just how much I love you. You take care of yourself and Dad."

Puzzled, she asked, "You will be home next week won't you?"

Dean groaned inwardly as he told his mother one last lie, "Oh, yeah, Mom, yeah. We will all see you soon. Love you. Bye, Mom." He hung up the phone quickly because he was losing control. He broke down. Karla put her arm around him. She knew that a similar call from her right away would be suspicious. She wouldn't get to say a word. Dean hadn't dealt with this part of the plan. They held each other and sobbed.

Dean managed to calm himself. James Dean walked up. Dean wrapped his massive arms around his father and held him close a long while. Then he put his hands on his Dad's shoulders, looked him in the eyes, gathered his usual spunk, and said, "Dad, everything's fine. The plan is fine. You and Mom are gonna be fine. And you know my Karla is so fine." For his father's sake, Dean straightened, saluted him, and walked arm in arm with Karla to the entrance of R-Team III.

James Dean watched them walk bravely away then pulled out his handkerchief. He never claimed to be tough. He turned and exited into an atrium; escalators there rose to three different businesses off Pennsylvania Avenue. He took the one that rose to a barber shop. He stayed for a trim and shine then stuffed his wet handkerchief back into his pocket.

Chapter 16

Dean and Karla entered a room plated with wall-to-wall electronics. Computers, copiers, laminators, cameras, video cameras, monitors, and tape recorders surrounded them. The remakers in R-Team III greeted Dean and Karla unemotionally. They were all business.

Dean's penchant for acting had gained him a fifteen-year assignment as Facilitator and Activator; now he would experience Renaissance. R-Team III was a flurry of activity the rest of that day and the next as Dean and Karla immersed themselves in new personas. The training was exhaustive. Details were deeply planted in their minds to achieve complete metamorphosis; this change was permanent.

They spent two nights in the hotel in conjunction with the changeover. A private elevator took them directly from R-Team III to a penthouse atop the building. At first sight of their quarters, Karla caught her breath. She had heard of Five-Star hotels; she was sure this qualified. The suite was luxurious and spacious—an oversized bedroom and bath, sitting room, and private dining area with flawless décor and original artwork. A balcony accessible from each area fronted the entire space. The balcony with its panoramic view of the city was Karla's greatest delight. That is, until waiters in tuxedos arrived to attend them with all the amenities of the posh restaurant floors below. She teased Dean that he outdid himself in planning their time in D.C. He gave her a knowing wink.

The two talked throughout the evenings. They discussed their training, their families, and their hopes and plans for the adventure before them. They role-played their new personas. They laughed. They cried. They dreamed out loud.

Dean told her the truth about each of his stories. He elaborated on how Padna's situation played out.

"Padna parachuted to safety just before the plane crash and was picked up by helicopter and delivered to Fort Riley Army Post at Junction City, Kansas, for safe-keeping. On the morning of the trial, he was dropped off at a local hospital and brought to the courthouse by ambulance, where he remained until time to testify. Seating a jury took only two hours; both attorneys moved to get the trial over quickly. The case for the defense was based on the mistaken idea that Padna died in Lake Ouachita. When the prosecutor called him to the witness stand, there was considerable stir on the other side of the room.

Padna's testimony established strong circumstantial evidence. What he said was backed up by documents— each signed by one of the accused—and supplemented with email and phone records. Upon leaving the stand, he faked a heart attack and was taken from the building on a stretcher to the same ambulance in which he had arrived. He changed clothes en route to the hospital, where he waited for the trial's outcome.

The defense attorneys were well prepared, skilled, and tenacious. They were also gracious in losing the case. After two hours on the second afternoon of the trial, the jury came to a unanimous verdict: Guilty! Padna took one last helicopter ride to a new life.

I still can't get the behavior of Bubba and Dubba Bubba. I thought I knew those guys. We went through some tough times together. They were a big disappointment. They must have really needed money. I don't know what happened to them. But I'll bet their real payday came when their St. Louis connection learned they slipped up."

"Now I understand why you seemed so bothered when I asked about Jamie Fox."

"You really threw me a curve. I was afraid someone had figured out he was involved and was pumping you for information. Actually, he synchronized assignment adjustments on Tuesdays. And, do you know why I always had an early breakfast at the diner every Wednesday morning? I had to meet with an informant. He did vehicle tracking for me on Tuesdays as a security double check for the agents involved."

He explained—to the degree he understood—how the many accidents had been staged. He described the Bridge work behind the scene and their meticulous development of details for each scenario.

Karla wasn't satisfied. "I don't see how you pulled off those complicated shell games with people's lives."

"That's why I went to D.C. continually. I had to have major interface in the logistics for all the different plans."

"Well, I don't know of any technologies that could keep people safe through those real life traumas."

"That always mystified me. The things they pulled off were better than science fiction. All I know is that the Bridge was privy to top secret chemical discoveries, materials from NASA, and computer design applications that are still not released for public use."

"I can *understand* why they are still secret. Our government needs tricks like that for operations at home and all around the world."

As the layers of mystery peeled away, Karla saw clearly the man she had chosen, the one she had chosen to believe regardless. She loved him even more.

"Karla, the thing that bothered me most all these years was the pain I caused you. I couldn't stand having you think I was messing with other women. That cheapened my relationship with you. And I hated you thinking I couldn't keep my hands off the bottle. You must have seen the real me way back at some point, or you wouldn't have put up with my shenanigans. I am so sorry for how you have been hurt. Please forgive me for a lifetime of lies."

"Of course, I forgive you. I can't say I never got angry. There were times I wanted to tear you limb from limb. But I sensed that deep down you loved me. You just had a lousy way of showing it. And I decided a long time ago that I love you. I wasn't going anywhere."

"That's what amazes me. I am so glad you stuck with me. And you didn't go around with a grudge. You have always been there for me. You never caved when I needed you."

Not once did they tire of talking. Sheer exhaustion forced them to sleep.

Chapter 17

At last, the training checklists were complete, and officials accompanied them to the Cessna XLT 170. Dean got last minute confirmation about flight instructions, and the doors were shut. Their helicopter lifted off and they sped over city after city.

For Karla, everything seemed surreal, while Dean seemed to be reveling in the experience. Sitting in the co-pilot's chair, she was so tense she could hardly speak. She rehearsed her fears. Finally, she asked, "Dean, do you remember that first computer you installed in the bank?"

He looked at her, incredulous. "For heaven's sake, Karla, of course I do! How often does a bank credit a one hundred dollar deposit as one hundred thousand dollars and have to go to court to get the money back? That mistake alone cost us over twenty-three thousand dollars in legal fees, transportation costs, and communications expenses.

"Well, what if the same guy wrote this program? If it's off like the bank's first one, we'll end up in the ocean."

He reassured her in his usual cavalier style. He grabbed her hand and said, "Hey, I land on my feet every time, Karla. This computer's fine, the weather's fine, and . . . ."

But she couldn't relax. She managed a weak smile and said, "Yes, I know. I'll be okay."

Soon, the aircraft carrier came in view. From the pilot's seat, Dean said, "Just watch this little baby handle the approach. I ain't gonna touch a thang." He lightly patted the computer.

The first signal of an incoming aircraft surprised the deck crew, still at breakfast. Orange lights lit up first. A split second later, red ones flashed in the corners of the mess hall—just before loud electronic whoops began. Flash! Flash! Whoop! Whoop! Whoop! Each continued for an entire minute. Stations were quickly manned in picture-perfect precision.

The crew of one hundred was skilled in international diversion, escape, rescue, and intervention; they were constantly on alert. The carrier, cruising eighty miles off the coast of Florida, was one of a fleet of autonomously managed vessels whose single purpose was to provide safety for the executive branch of Government. The crew was not given advance notice about assignments. But two weeks of drills had told them to be ready for impending duties.

The incoming aircraft radioed that they were below three thousand feet about twelve miles out and closing at one hundred seventy knots. Two signal crewmen were set and waiting, cables in place at the Alpha, Beta and Omega positions. One asked the other, "Did I hear correctly? Is this thing coming in at one hundred seventy?"

"That's what he said. I was expecting something a little more breakneck—like a Stealth at six hundred."

Suddenly there was another announcement, "Second aircraft approaching! Twelve miles out, two hundred feet and holding, speed one hundred seventy." The second alert caught them off guard. Two aircraft were approaching at relatively low speed.

"What do you suppose they are?"

"I'd say bi-planes or helicopters."

His second guess was correct. The Cessna XLT170 approached the aircraft carrier at ninety knots and synchronized its speed with the carrier's twenty-two knots. The approach was perfect, the landing textbook. The Cessna was little work for the crewmen, requiring just "Straight ahead! Hold!"

The second helicopter approached seconds later and hovered off deck for last minute clearance. The second aircraft was *the big green helicopter.* This unique design, in use from 1980 until past 1995, was not chronicled in the media, libraries, or congressional record. This helicopter which did not officially exist would provide the last ride for Dean and Karla Story. This pick-up by the green machine was critical to success of the program. Bridge leaders accepted nothing short of perfection.

The word came. "Project affirmative: pick up passengers. Destination: moving van." The generic message was code—nothing special, nothing revealing— and could have been safely sent over the radio.

The media would report a crash of the Cessna XLT170, though it landed safely on the carrier. This would not create conflict for the crew. The passengers of that helicopter wouldn't be remotely tied to their ship in the Atlantic. The day's events easily masqueraded as a trial exercise, merely a practice run—the people involved, actors. The ship's log bore a nondescript entry for the day's exercise: "Cessna XLT170 checked and put in hold. Passengers safely aboard green machine, sixteen minutes on destination to intercept moving van."

The crew had no idea they had facilitated the end of Grayville's Story. Karla would receive no more phone calls about Dean and felony charges. James Dean would hand out fewer greenbacks for legal fees, motel bills, car rentals, airline tickets, and bail. This was the demise of a prime source of news and gossip. A truly interesting character was being consigned to memories and *good-times* stories told in hunting clubs in Arkansas, Colorado, Texas, and Montana.

As the green helicopter flew across the ocean, Dean and Karla sat quiet, staring straight ahead. Neither could fully relax, and they were silent a long while. To think, "What if . . . ." was agonizing. When Karla finally turned to Dean, he could see her concern. She whispered, "Dean, I didn't sleep well last night. I couldn't get my brother and sister off my mind. Do you think there's any way I could check on them in a few months?"

He couldn't flinch. He had bet his life that the contract would be honored. He had to demonstrate the resolve required of them both. "Don't you think that would violate the trust between us and BDI?"

Tears were filling her eyes. She realized what he was saying. She nodded. "You're right. I vowed. That makes the contract binding, and I know that. I still hurt, Dean. They're my only living blood relatives."

Dean's eyes betrayed his own struggle as he looked at her. "I know, Karla. This is almost too painful for me, too. I do understand. I'm counting on you. You count on me. We will lean on each other. I'll be here whenever you need reassurance." He cupped her hand in his then leaned over and kissed her gently. "I am not your blood relative. But I am your covenant relative. We are in this together."

138

She looked back at him. Tears were now running down her cheeks. "Dean, I said, 'I do,' once before. I haven't changed my mind. I still do." She smiled in defiance of her tears.

They reached their destination. The large green helicopter stopped squarely on the landing pad. The co-pilot shouted over the deafening *whir* of the blades, "Wait here. The loading ramp will be brought out and connected directly to the Moving Van." The plane sitting nearby was the Moving Van; the name came from its first passenger, Jake Tullis, Dean's old roommate. The BDI Bridge had staffed it from Day One and proudly served all its passengers. The ramp moved into place. The co-pilot gave the signal, "All clear. You may board."

Dean and Karla rose from their seats. He reached and pulled her close. He held her a long minute and gently kissed her forehead. He whispered, "Ready?" She nodded. Together they took a deep breath of excitement and walked hand in hand across the ramp.